YOUR LIVES
IN OUR HANDS

(Based on true stories from a retired hospital doctor)

Dr Jay

To my wife, herself a doctor, who looked after my two kids when I was doing a 'one in two' on call rota as a Surgical registrar.

CONTENTS

PREFACE

I am a sixty-six year old debut author. Increasing age has not diminished my curiosity to listen to a story or eagerness to tell a story.

Now that I am a retired doctor I am free from the shackles of targets, deadlines and other constraints on my time. I have had the luxury of looking back on my career in the NHS and writing down a few memorable experiences. These episodes are based on my recollections of incidents that occurred when I was on call for surgical emergencies or when I was doing outpatient clinics. Numerous similar incidents do happen in hospitals up and down the country. The names of patients and doctors in these stories have been changed to protect their identites.

All the stories described have something unusual and remarkable about them that I remember them vividly and want to share them with the general public, who I hope, will have the inquisitiveness to read them all.

The dividing line between fiction and reality can be blurred and indistinguishable. For example, the bizarre cases of removed foreign bodies, the paint brush, the vibrator and the jam jar, may sound entirely fictional and unbelievable, but they are based on true stories. I have also described several rare clinical cases like the spontaneous rupture of the gullet and spontaneous rupture of a tumour of the liver.

I have tried to give the reader an insider's description of what I have done or witnessed or just come across during my years of practice in NHS hospitals in England and Wales. Some of the stories are about people who were in precarious and vulnerable situations who came through safe and well. For example there is the unusual case of the hundred-and-one year old lady who overcame her surgical ordeal with great aplomb. There is the story of the six-week-old baby who had a rare congenital condition and had to be sent urgently to a specialist centre. However, there is also the story of a young man involved in a motor bike accident which left me heartbroken. We doctors often put on a brave face in front of relatives of patients but we also are human beings who go through emotional turmoil when our patients don't do well.

I have attempted to avoid prejudice of any sort from these stories. Even though I may have highlighted the behaviour and attitudes of some colleagues as less than satisfactory, I do believe that they were all clinicians who were doing their best for patients on most other occasions. This book is not an exercise in 'whistle blowing' but it doesn't whitewash or conceal short comings either. *Nobody has a monopoly on virtue but failings have to be recognised and corrected to avoid compromising the safety of patients.*

There have been tremendous improvements in facilities and equipment since I worked as a junior doctor thirty-odd years ago when most of these stories happened. The story of the young child who was thrown through the windscreen of a car highlights the struggle we had faced due to lack of an essential investigative tool, a CT scan.

The title of the book, *Your Lives In Our Hands* is not meant to alarm the reader. It is simply to emphasise the magnitude of the responsibility the doctors shoulder every day. The stories of the child with the head injury, the boy kicked by a pony, the gentleman who had internal strangulation of small bowel, the young lady who fell off the horse and many other stories described in this book prove the point.

THE CENTURION WHO DIDN'T MIND BEING CALLED JENNY

My bleep, or bleeper as some would call it, was continually wailing all day, that day. Mind you, that was the case most days because I was working as a Surgical Registrar without support of a Senior House Officer. (There was no Senior House Officer post in General Surgery in that hospital). This incident took place about twenty-eight years ago in a hospital in England. There were five Pre-Registration House officers who were fresh graduates, coming straight from Medical School for their first job as a doctor. The fact that there was no Senior House Officer made the job of the Surgical Registrar incredibly busy. The Registrar was the only one the new House Officers could turn to if they couldn't insert a cannula into a patient's vein (required for the administration of medication or replacement of fluid) or even take routine blood samples from a patient.

The Registrars employed were fairly senior and well experienced. The Consultant Surgeons, three of the five, were looking forward to their retirement in a year or two. They left the Registrar to get on with most surgical emergencies, unless their presence in theatre was absolutely essential. There were only two Registrars for five Consultant Surgeons and the workload was immense – we were expected to be on-call (working twenty-four hours continuously) every other day and every other weekend – a so-called 'one in two' on-call rota. Today, that arrangement would be illegal because of the exhaustive and punishing schedule. Registrar was not

3

first on call and the House officers took all the calls from the General Practitioners (GPs, known as family doctors in some countries) who were referring patients to the hospital for admission as surgical emergencies

That day Richard, the House officer attached to Mr Chung, Consultant General Surgeon, was on the phone when I answered the bleep. He said that a GP was on the phone and that he wanted to speak to me personally and was insisting that it may not be a patient referral for admission.

When I took the call and asked the GP what it was all about, he was rather apologetic and said to me, "One of my patients is in a bit of bother. I am not sure what to do. The patient is a hundred and one years of age. In spite of her age, she lives alone because she has some home help. She was very well except for the sudden onset of some ailment which has left her in a lot of pain. I could, of course, leave her with plenty of painkillers if a surgeon decided that she would not be a suitable case for surgery. I must emphasise that this woman has been in reasonably good health despite her age."

I felt that it was genuine, albeit hesitant, call from a caring medical practitioner.

If the grand old lady had a true surgical emergency, he wanted an opinion from a surgeon before deciding her fate and leaving her in the lap of the Gods, with plenty of painkillers. The GP knew fully well that, in those days, most Surgeons wouldn't consider touching this lady with a 'surgical barge pole'. That was why he was apologetic in the tone of his conversation.

I didn't take too long to answer the man. I told him I could make a decision only after seeing the patient myself. "Please send the lady to the surgical ward to avoid the delay in admitting her through the A/E (Accident and Emergency) Department."

In the 1970s and 80s Consultant Surgeons would leave Surgical Registrars to shoulder a huge chunk of responsibility. These were the days before the CEPOD (Confidential Enquiry into Peri-Operative Deaths) report which challenged the Consultants to be more proactive. To be fair to them, let us say that the majority of Consultants were confident that the Registrars appointed to these posts were senior and experienced enough to handle emergencies themselves. It is also true that if the Consultant came to do every emergency operation, the Registrar wouldn't acquire sufficient experience to become a Consultant.

When the ward informed me about the arrival of the patient I had accepted, I went and saw her in the ward, the surgical House Officer Richard in tow. I introduced myself to the lady who, in spite of her age and her predicament, looked remarkably well turned out! She had her hair, her face make up and her lipstick all in order. I wondered how she managed to get herself presentable in the time an ambulance made its way to her house where she lived alone. I could see that she was in considerable pain. When I asked her to tell me about herself and how come she was there in the hospital, she managed a naughty smile and said to me, "My name is Jennifer, but if you want to call me Jenny - I don't mind!"

I must admit that with that answer, at a stroke, she lightened the atmosphere. She added that she was a retired Ward Sister and that she was not intimidated by hospitals or doctors. I was reminded of the Matron in the *Carry On Doctor* film even though Jennifer was a thinner lady. I went on to examine her very gently and carefully (with the due respect for a retired Ward Sister).

She had board-like rigidity of the abdomen with tenderness on palpation. I strongly suspected that she had a perforated organ in her abdomen because she had all the signs and symptoms of acute peritonitis (inflammation of the sac covering the abdominal contents). The diagnosis was largely dependent on the patient's story and the examination findings of the doctor. A plain X-ray of the abdomen would show air under the diaphragm on the right side in most cases of perforated bowel but even if the X-ray was inconclusive, the patient's history and the clinical findings would make a compelling case for surgical exploration.

When I was examining her, she said, "Whatever happened to me was abrupt. I was on a chair simply watching television when I felt the sudden severe pain in my tummy." She did not give a clear history of symptoms suggestive of peptic ulcer even when I probed her. She didn't have any sign of age-related loss of memory. Often patients are dismissive of their symptoms and clinicians are aware of this. She was a smoker for a long time but had stopped smoking a couple of years ago (smoking is one of the causes for peptic ulcer).

I told the lady, "My impression is that most likely you have burst an ulcer in your tummy and only an exploration of the abdomen by an operation will show us what exactly the problem is." I added, "If it is a perforation of an ulcer on the small bowel, I could repair it quickly, but if it is the large bowel it will take more time and you may end up with a colostomy bag (to collect bowel contents diverted through an artificial opening the surgeon makes on the abdominal wall)."

She knew what a colostomy bag was, having been a nurse herself. Her response was, "I cannot go on like this, can I? Do whatever you need to do.

If I have to have a colostomy bag so be it. I will be in good company. The Queen Mother apparently has one."

I knew that a number of Surgeons told their patients that the Queen Mother had a colostomy bag in the hope of softening the blow for the patients when they are told about the necessity of a colostomy. I have no idea whether it is just a ploy by the Surgeons or a true statement.

The answer this lady gave me was poignant. "I cannot go on like this, can I?" In it she made quite clear that she wanted to go on. She did not want to end everything then and there with the help of some pain relief. I made up my mind.

When the Anaesthetist heard that an old lady of a hundred and one years was to have an emergency laparotomy he asked me, "Are you having a laugh? Is that supposed to be a joke?" He asked me if I had spoken to Mr Chung, the Consultant on call. I reminded him that Mr Chung was not particularly keen on leaving the comfort of his home to do a laparotomy if he could avoid it and that he would simply agree with my clinical judgement. However, I said I would try to get hold of him and tell him of my decision about the lady.

The theatre staff were always helpful. Their cooperation was essential for any Surgical Registrar on call, doing emergency operations every other day and night and every other week end. Obviously, one or two eye balls may have rolled upwards behind my back when the age of the patient was mentioned by the anaesthetist or the House Officer who booked the case on the emergency operation list.

Jennifer was lucky. It was only a perforated duodenal ulcer, an ulcer on the first part of the intestine. I managed to close the perforation, with a patch of omentum (the frill of the stomach) over the ulcer, wash out the contaminated abdominal cavity with warm saline (salt water), insert a small drain in the abdomen and close the laparotomy wound as fast as I could. The Anaesthetist had already given her the appropriate antibiotic prophylaxis to prevent any post-operative infection.

She was very pleased that she did not join the company of the famous people with colostomies. Having been a nurse herself several years ago she knew what a colostomy was like and she was pleased to have avoided it, even though she had consented to it if it had been necessary. She had an uneventful recovery and was discharged to a convalescence home after twelve days, having been kept in hospital for a couple more days than usual.

Three months later I met Mr Chung in the corridor of the hospital after he had finished a very busy clinic. He said, "Guess whom I had the pleasure of seeing in the clinic today! The hundred-and-one year old lady you had operated on three months ago. She came for a routine follow up. She was absolutely fine."

"Mr Chung," I told him. "You made my day! Isn't it wonderful news? I believe that the chronological age of a patient, by itself, should not be a contra-indication to surgical intervention if the patient's life is in danger."

"Absolutely," he agreed.

THE BOY WHO GOT KICKED BY HIS BROTHER'S PONY

I had just finished my two-year contract as a Surgical Registrar in a hospital in England. The next available job was that of a locum Registrar in Surgery for six months in a hospital not too far away. I was pleased that I could stay at home with my family even though it was not a more substantial or longer term job.

The trouble with doing a locum job, especially in Surgery as a Registrar, is that most of the staff you have to work with initially look at you with suspicion. They have not seen you or worked with you before. If you happen to be a foreign graduate, especially a brown or black guy, the index of prejudice and the lack of confidence is very high. Of course one tries to wield one's charm and get people to like one by being polite to everybody and being friendly and pleasant. In spite of all that, there will be some who will never trust the foreign doctor, especially if he is a locum, an unknown quantity.

There were only three Registrars in Surgery at that busy hospital but there were three Senior House Officers to support us in addition to the Pre-Registration House Officers. The children's hospital was about three miles away. Fairly small operations on children, like removing the appendix, had to be performed there. There was no Paediatric Surgeon on call and the General Surgery Registrar and Consultant on call in the main hospital covered the surgical emergencies for children. Any major procedures on children had to be done in the main hospital theatres, not in the children's hospital.

The Senior House Officer (SHO) working with me that night, Neal, was an experienced, hard-working guy from Birmingham, who had impressed me as a capable SHO when he was on call with me the previous week.

He telephoned me. "I have been called to see a five-year-old boy in the Accident and Emergency Department who was kicked by a pony. Apparently the boy loved his brother's pony and tried to kiss the animal, which used its hind leg and kicked him on his tummy to record its disapproval."

I said that I would meet him in the A/E straight away.

When I saw the boy he was rather tired of all the attention and he was keen to go home but he allowed me to examine him. There was a bruise on the front of the abdomen on the right side just below the lower rib margin over the area of the liver. Children do at times resent any examination and even though he had agreed that I could examine him, he started to cry. It was quite obvious that he didn't like my hand over his tummy. I had made sure that my hands were made warm by placing them on the radiator before I touched him but that didn't make any difference. The SHO had already examined him and I could easily see that he had some pain when he was being examined. There were worrying signs of an acute abdomen, like guarding and rebound tenderness, even after allowing for some margin of error during the examination of a weary and resentful child.

The mother was expecting an 'all clear' from me and was hopeful that she could take the child home. When I told her that the child needed an operation she was upset as well as very sceptical. I explained to her that the clinical signs on physical examination were highly suspicious of an internal injury and that it was dangerous to be complacent and do nothing, in anticipation that the boy would be all right after a while. I asked the SHO to arrange essential preoperative blood tests and inform the anaesthetist on call to come and see the child before booking a laparotomy (surgical exploration of abdomen) in the main theatre.

After about an hour I had a call from the A/E. The SHO, Neal, was on the phone again.

"The Sister in charge of A/E was unhappy with your diagnosis and she got the Casualty Consultant involved. Apparently the Consultant said that an Ultrasound should be done and that the child could go home if it was all right. The Ultrasound was done and it did not show any abnormality in the abdomen and the mother of the child is keen to take him home. Sister wants you to come to A/E and discharge the child."

Thankfully I was not too busy with other emergencies that day and I made my way to the A/E. The Sister in charge had not met me previously. She had steely eyes and a hostile attitude towards me. She simply told me, "The Ultrasound suggested by the A/E Consultant turned out to be normal. The child's mother wants to take the child home. She has other children to take care of. The neighbour is looking after them at present. I think you should discharge the child."

The Senior Registrar in Anaesthesia had already seen the child because the SHO had booked the case in theatre for a laparotomy. She had completed her training and was looking for a Consultant post. She was present during my conversation with the Sister and was fully supportive of the Sister. She said, "The child is just irritated because it is past his bed time and he should be allowed home. The ultrasound is normal anyway!"

Obviously the Anaesthetist was not very pleased about putting a child to sleep for a procedure and if the case was cancelled it would be one case less for her to do that night. One should remember that the Anaesthetist on call has to anaesthetise all patients for operations whether they are for Surgical, Orthopaedic, Gynaecological or for any other speciality.

This was a tricky situation. The Sister in charge of A/E has joined forces with the Anaesthetist to ignore my opinion and pressurise me to change my mind and send the child home.

I told both the honourable ladies respectfully but firmly, "On the basis of my examination I suspect an internal injury in this child which may not be evident on an Ultrasound scan. Unfortunately we don't have a CT scan in the hospital and Ultrasound is notoriously unreliable. I am not prepared to discharge him."

Not surprisingly, the mother of the child was rather resentful and confused. She just wanted to take the child home if it was possible, especially after listening to conflicting opinions from two different doctors, one of them saying that the child should be allowed home.

I was in need of support and back up.

I telephoned Mr Marshall, the Consultant Surgeon on call and explained the situation. I was planning to speak to him in any case, before taking the child to theatre. He listened to me carefully and told me to go ahead and do the operation and that he would try and come as well. I explained the conversation I had with Mr Marshall to the boy's mother and got her to sign the consent form.

The A/E Sister had no choice but to instruct the nurses to prepare the child for theatre. He was kept starving since he was first seen in A/E and was soon wheeled into the theatre and the anaesthetic room.

When I was scrubbing up, Neal was also scrubbing up to assist me in theatre. He was furious and he kept saying that the Anaesthetist had no business to interfere and say the things she had said in presence of the child's mother. I kept quiet but silently agreed with him. I was also quite tensed up wondering what the findings would be, even though I was convinced that there were signs of peritonitis (inflammation of the thin sac enveloping the contents of abdomen) and that an internal injury had to be ruled out. However, I was also apprehensive especially after the whole drama in A/E.

When I placed a mid-line incision in the upper abdomen of the child, the Anaesthetist leant forward over the head of the child and looked. When I opened the peritoneum, the sac covering the abdominal contents, she gleefully commented, "I don't see any blood gushing out."

This was a put down, intended to tell me that she was right all along and that there was nothing wrong with the child.

I was quite weary of the continual sniping from this lady. I looked at her without any effort to hide my displeasure and told her sternly, "You make sure that the child is sleeping when I am doing the operation." The tone of my voice and the menace in my glance at her put a stop to any further comments. Carefully, I extended the incision on the peritoneum. Lo and behold! There was bile and intestinal contents emerging mixed with peritoneal fluid suggesting that there was perforation of the bowel. Further careful inspection revealed a 'punch-hole' perforation of the jejunum, the second part of the small intestine.

Blunt abdominal injuries are known to cause this type of perforation. I have had the experience of operating on two people previously where the clinical presentation was blunt abdominal injury and finding on operation was punch-hole perforation of the intestine.

I heard the creaking sound of the theatre door opening and MrMarshall asking, "What did you find? Was it the liver?"

I said that it was not the liver and explained the finding to him.

He had not changed into a theatre gown. "All right then. See you. Bye."

I closed the perforation with vicryl sutures, washed out the peritoneal cavity with normal saline, placed a small vacuum drain in place in the abdomen and finished the operation. Appropriate antibiotic prophylaxis was already given by the anaesthetist as per my request. She was only too willing to help. She was quite silent and I suspect a wee bit remorseful of her earlier conduct.

Neal declared rather loudly, "Well done Mr Jay. If it were not for your prompt diagnosis and the courage of your conviction, this child would have been allowed home and he would have probably died."

Again there was stony silence from the head end of the operation table where the Anaesthetist was seated.

THE PAINT BRUSH, THE VIBRATOR AND THE JAM JAR

The Paint Brush

I was the Surgical Registrar on call in that hospital that day, covering Urological emergencies as well. Usually common Urological problems seen in the Accident and Emergency Department are retention of urine, blocked indwelling catheters, renal or ureteric colic from kidney stones and suspected torsions of testes. Occasionally someone who got the tip of his foreskin caught in the zip of his trousers (because he was not wearing his underpants) or similar other cases may also present themselves to Casualty.

This case was totally different and unexpected. The Senior House Officer (SHO) in Accident and Emergency Department (A/E) asked me to see a thirty-five year old man who had pushed a very thin paint brush up inside his penis. His hobby was painting pictures and the small dry paint brush was one he had used several times in the past during painting. Why he did what he did was not something he was prepared to talk about. That was an issue for him during a later consultation with a psychosexual counsellor or a psychiatrist. The problem was that when he withdrew the brush from the penis, the bristles and the small ring holding them together got stuck in the urethra (the natural pipe through which a man's urine comes out). Only the handle of the brush, the size of a pencil, came out and it was intact, according to him. He did not bring it with him.

13

When I saw him he seemed a normal-looking thirty-five year old - fairly tall, thin - who was quite cooperative. He said that he was unmarried and that he had no girlfriends or partners. He had no previous urological problems. There was no history of any sexually transmitted diseases or any other serious illness in the past.

On examining him, there was no bleeding at the tip of the penis. There was no abnormality to see. I had to make sure that the story was not a hoax. I asked the man, "Is it true that you pushed the paint brush up into your penis?"

He said, "Yes. Only the handle came out when I tried to take the brush back."

I explained to him, "It is necessary for us to have a look with a telescope up the pipe (the urethra) under general anaesthesia to see if it is possible to remove what was left behind with a forceps. If that attempt fails an open operation may be necessary."

The written consent was obtained and he was prepared for theatre.

The Consultant Surgeon on call that night, Mr Al-Mulaly, was a doing a locum in place of Mr Knight. He was a General Surgeon and was not very experienced in endoscopic urological procedures. When I rang him at home to tell him about the case he asked me, "Are you confident to do the case?"

I answered, "Yes."

"All right then. Go ahead. If you can't take it out, we may have to do open surgery. Give me a ring and let me know," Mr Al-Mulaly instructed.

The night duty nursing staff in theatre were very friendly colleagues with whom I had worked for more than eighteen months, every other night. They were willing to help any way they could. The only problem was that many of them were unfamiliar with endoscopic urological instruments, having worked mainly at night and not having done any elective Urological operation lists. That meant that I had to select and assemble the instruments myself during the procedure.

Carefully I inspected the urethra with the telescope. My main concern was whether the bristles were all loose and spread around which would make it very difficult, almost impossible, to get them out at one go. Thankfully the metal ring holding the bristles together was intact. I did manage a sigh of relief and said, "Thank God for that" and I meant it.

After visualising the object lodged in the urethra and holding the Cystoscope (the telescope with which urethra and bladder are inspected) in the correct position I asked the nurse for the grabbing forceps which I could insert through the scope to grab and remove it. Bless her, she didn't know what I was asking for and gave me something else instead. Then I had to take the telescope out and return to the trolley again. After the helper nurse called the 'runner' brought several trays, I managed to spot the forceps that was needed. I went back in to the urethra with the scope and the grabber. The part of the paint brush which had taken residence in the man's urethra was gently removed. I was genuinely pleased that the man was spared an open surgical procedure on his urethra which could have resulted in further complications. (Open operations on the urethra are notorious for subsequent complications.) He was given prophylactic antibiotics and discharged home the next day.

He had refused a consultation with psychosexual counsellor even though it was offered.

The Vibrator

This is the case of a respectable fifty-six year old company director who went to the A/E and divulged the information that a vibrator found its way up his back passage during some sex game he and his wife were engaged in and that they couldn't retrieve it.

When the SHO in A/E telephoned me and referred the case to me, the on call Surgical Registrar, I thought he was playing some sort of practical joke on me. To be honest, I did not know what a vibrator was. Call me naïve, call me stupid, but thirty years ago I simply didn't know what it was. After a brief conversation with the Surgical HO working with me that day who explained to me what a vibrator was, I made way to the A/E to see the patient.

The patient, a well-dressed, seemingly respectable man, looked peevish and was apologetic. He repeated his story. The vibrator was a battery operated cylindrical device the size of a large pen torch and during their sexual adventures it found its way up his rectum according to him. It was no longer active because the battery had run out but they couldn't remove it.

I asked him, "Would you let me examine you with a sigmoidoscope, which is a telescope with which the back passage can be inspected? I could attempt to remove it here in the casualty Department itself so that you wouldn't need to undergo a procedure under general anaesthesia."

He was very pleased with my suggestion.

The sigmoidoscope was brought from theatre, together with the appropriate grabbing device. The patient was most cooperative. Alas! The device was wedged transversely and it was impossible to remove it then and there. The patient was also in some discomfort even though he was quite stoic and uncomplaining.

After obtaining his consent for a procedure under GA (general anaesthesia) he was taken to the main theatre. Under general anaesthesia he was more relaxed and I managed to remove the rogue vibrator easily. He was given prophylactic antibiotics.

The patient was relieved that the embarrassing episode was over. He was admitted for observation overnight but when I attended ward rounds the next day he was nowhere to be seen. The nurses told me that he discharged himself in the early hours of the morning. I was also told that the address he had given and the details of his next of kin were all false!

The Jam Jar

The third case is the story of the jam jar. This was in a hospital about fifty miles away from where the previous cases I described took place. When I was told by the Surgical SHO on call with me that evening that there was a guy in A/E who pushed a jam jar up his back passage which got stuck high up in the rectum, it sounded bizarre. I was not too surprised because I already had the strange experience of taking out two objects one from the urethra (urine pipe) and the other from the rectum (back passage). The jam jar was by far the largest device of the lot. I was told that the lid was screwed in and tight.

'That will make it difficult to grab it with a pair of grabbing forceps,' I thought to myself.

That day I was assisting the Consultant Surgeon on call, MrParker, in his elective surgical operation list at the general hospital three miles away from the main hospital where the man with the jar had presented himself in the A/E.

When I told him about the jam jar, in between cases, he said to me, "I shall finish the remaining cases here. You go and sort out the emergency. Do it under general anaesthesia."

I telephoned the SHO and asked him to arrange the theatre and anaesthetist.

When I saw him I did not ask the man how or why a jam jar ended up where it was stuck. He was rather expressionless during our conversation. I explained to him the possibility of rectal injury while trying to remove the jar and asked him for the consent for an abdominal operation if it was necessary. The patient agreed without any hesitation.

To remove the jar from below was impossible in spite of all my valiant efforts. I even tried using a vacuum device commonly used to deliver babies during difficult labour cases. Every time I tried it, the rectal wall got entangled and there was a high risk of rectal injury. A rectal perforation would have necessitated a colostomy, at least temporarily.

As I was sweating and struggling without any success, Mr Parker arrived after finishing the routine operation list in the General Hospital. He said he would like to have one attempt himself. He did try but soon he realised that removing it from below without manipulating it from above was impossible. He asked me to scrub up and open the abdomen and gently apply pressure from above when he would pull from below.

I did precisely what Mr Parker suggested.

With the SHO assisting me, I did a laparotomy and gently managed to dislodge the jar from above. Subsequently Mr Parker successfully removed the jam jar from below. The patient had the appropriate antibiotic prophylaxis during the procedure

The post-operative period was uneventful. The man was pleased that rectal injury was avoided and that he didn't end up with a colostomy bag. He was discharged home after seven days in hospital. He declined an appointment with a Psychiatrist.

It was a pity that the three men whom I have described above refused any follow up consultation with a Psycho-sexual counsellor or a Psychiatrist. It is true that you can only lead a horse to the stream; you cannot make it drink the water!

THE BABY WHO CRIED INTERMITTENTLY

It was in 1983, in between my regular jobs, that I did a two weeks' locum job as a Senior House Officer (SHO) in a teaching hospital in the City of London. That was the only time I ever worked in a hospital in the heart of the great city.

The job was to work with a famous Professor of Urology and during on call duties I had to cover General Surgical emergencies. I was very happy that I got an opportunity to work with the Professor. Alas! When I got there I found that the Professor was on leave for two weeks. I was very disappointed.

That evening when I was on call I was regularly being bleeped to see patients in the Accident and Emergency Department. Most of them were minor cases which were discharged after I had seen them because they did not need admission.

By about 8 p.m. I was called again by the SHO in A/E. He said, "Could you please come and see this child who cries intermittently. I have examined the child carefully. I cannot find anything wrong. Please come and have a look. You may be able to send the child home."

I made my way to the A/E again.

The 'child' he referred to me was a fourteen-month-old baby. A lovely little girl with a beautiful smile, she looked perfectly all right. Her mother, a young lady of Eastern European appearance, was holding the baby, and her boyfriend, who was not the baby's father, was standing very close to the mother almost cuddling her.

I asked the mother, "What happened? When did the baby start crying?"

"Nothing happened." She looked startled when she replied as if denying that she had done anything wrong to the baby. "This evening she started crying. I don't know why." As she was speaking, the baby gave a sudden cry of anguish. I was surprised. A baby who was smiling happily up to that time, suddenly cried out as if stung by something.

I took the baby from her mother's arms, placed her on a bed in the cubicle and examined her. She was looking at my eyes and face and smiling happily. She was not feverish; her temperature was entirely normal. All the observations done by the nurses before I came to see the baby were also normal. When I examined the baby the abdomen felt soft and unremarkable. There was no evidence of any tenderness anywhere. In fact, the baby felt ticklish when I was palpating her tummy and she started laughing! That little baby girl was the most happy and normal looking baby I was ever asked to see in a Casualty Department. All the time I was examining the baby, the mother was being kissed and petted and squeezed by her boyfriend and both of them were ecstatic in each other's company rather than sorry for an ill baby.

I gave the baby back to the mother and instantly she cried out in agony again. I was baffled as to what was happening! Was the mother intermittently pricking the baby with a needle kept in between her fingers? There was no obvious needle marks or bruises on the baby when I had examined her.

I telephoned the Senior Registrar on call with me and explained the situation. He said that he would also come and see the baby.

In the meantime, the mother and boyfriend were getting impatient with me. "What are you doing to check the baby out? Can you not see that the baby is not well? She needs to be admitted immediately. Can't you see she is crying, see!"

Again the baby cried out for a few seconds.

"The Senior Registrar, Mr Vaughn, is much more experienced than me. He will see the baby and decide what we have to do," I said.

They were not interested in the opinion of the Senior Registrar. "Whoever comes, it is obvious that the baby needs admission," the mother declared.

Thankfully, as we were engaged in this conversation Mr Vaughn arrived. He saw that the baby was a pleasant, normal looking baby. He couldn't find anything abnormal on examining the child. Nevertheless, he witnessed the intermittent cry of anguish from the baby when she was being held by the mother. Mr Vaughn was a very experienced Senior Registrar almost at the end of his long training programme. He surveyed the scene and immediately diagnosed the problem.

He said to the mother, choosing his words carefully, "Yes. I can see that the baby will be unwell if we let her go home. We will admit her to the ward. Come back tomorrow morning to the ward and see if the baby can be taken home."

I was a bit puzzled. "Why should we admit a normal looking child without any ailment to the children's ward with other sick children?" I said to myself.

The mother gave the baby's milk bottle and other belongings she had brought with her to the nurse and darted out of the A/E like a shot.

Mr Vaughn told me, "Dr Jay, that mother has found her new boyfriend and they want to go somewhere for a night out tonight. This baby is the hindrance. They want the baby to be looked after overnight. They know that the best place for the baby is the hospital. If we deny admission to this baby it may come to some harm tonight. That is why we should admit her to the ward. I didn't want to examine her fingers to see if she was pricking the baby with a needle," he continued. "That won't make an iota of change in the situation. Could you please arrange the admission of the child? Tell the nurses in the ward that the social workers should be informed of this admission."

I happily agreed and learnt a valuable lesson about human behaviour that night.

THE LADY WHO HAD A RUPTURED ECTOPIC PREGNANCY

The hospital in Wales where I had worked several years ago had no Gynaecological wing. All cases of Obstetrics and Gynaecology were dealt with in a separate hospital about three miles away. Very occasionally an ambulance will carry an emergency patient, in error, to the Accident and Emergency Department in the main hospital where I worked. Most of the time, the patient will be sent to the appropriate place in the same ambulance. Some General medical emergencies and children's admissions also were similarly sent to the appropriate hospitals nearby. The main hospital dealt with all the General Surgical emergencies.

One day when I was the on call Surgical Registrar, a twenty-two year old lady was brought to the main A/E in an ambulance. The Senior House Officer (SHO) in A/E who examined her thought that she probably had a surgical condition. He asked me for an opinion. There were no facilities for any investigation like an emergency Ultrasound scan and the nearest CT scan was in a neurology centre fifty miles away.

When I saw her she looked pale and quite unwell.

"What happened?" I asked.

She said that she felt a sudden severe pain in her lower abdomen and that she felt faint at that time. "Now I feel very tired and my tummy hurts and it looks a bit bigger than normal."

I asked her about her monthly periods and she said that she had a miscarriage the previous week and subsequently had undergone a D&C (Dilation and Curettage, usually done to remove any retained products of conception) in a private clinic in Cardiff. On examination her abdomen looked distended.

I asked, "Do you feel any discomfort in your shoulder?"

She seemed surprised that I knew that. (The pressure on the diaphragm from the blood distending the abdomen can cause a referred pain in the shoulder.)

"Yes," she said without hesitation.

On palpating her abdomen there were signs of peritonitis (inflammation of the thin sac covering abdominal contents) and the presence of free fluid in abdomen. The clinical picture was that of a ruptured ectopic pregnancy. I remembered the cases I had diagnosed and operated on when I was working in Nigeria in the seventies. The only confusing issue was the history of a D&C in a private clinic in Cardiff after an apparent miscarriage the previous week.

I made up my mind and said to myself, "This young lady has a ruptured ectopic pregnancy unless otherwise proved. This is a case for the Registrar in Gynaecology." I decided to contact him myself in case he declined to accept a referral from an SHO in A/E.

The Registrar in gynaecology based in the other hospital answered his bleep promptly. I explained the case to him clearly and informed him of my clinical impression. I also told him that it was unwise to move her to the other hospital in an ambulance because of the considerable risk of further bleeding in a young woman who is already anaemic. I said that I would like him or his Consultant to come over and do the laparotomy in the main hospital where I was. I told him that I would arrange the theatre and get the Anaesthetist to see the patient.

The response was swift and straight forward. He said, "We are not allowed to come and do any operation there in the main hospital. Mr Jones is the Consultant on call today. Why don't you ring him and ask him if he would come and see this woman?"

'That is interesting,' I thought.

Only few weeks ago the Gynaecologists had a lady with severe peritonitis from pelvic infection when I had to go over there and do an operation there as per their referral to General Surgeons. One rule for their Registrars and another rule for us, the Surgical Registrars!

Experience had taught me that barking up the wrong tree was not very wise or fruitful. There was no mileage in arguing with this guy. He has, not without reason, made clear why he was refusing to see this patient. Now it was up to me to sort out something for a young woman whose life could be in danger if an operation was delayed. I decided to ring Mr Jones, the Consultant Gynaecologist on call.

Soon I found out that Mr Jones was not a very obliging man to refer a patient to. He was cross with me, a mere Registrar in Surgery, who had dared to ring him directly instead of asking the Consultant Surgeon on call to contact him. He was quietly furious even though he didn't shout at me.

"Did your Consultant see this patient?" he asked me. When I said that he had not, Mr Jones was unequivocal in his pronouncement. "Get him to see the patient and ask him to ring me."

Without wasting time I rang Mr Humphrey, the Consultant Surgeon on call and explained the predicament of this young lady. I made clear that I was very reluctant to send her in the ambulance for another journey and expose her to the risk of further bleeding internally. For some reason Mr Humphrey did not ring Mr Jones, his colleague, to discuss this. He lived fifteen miles away and he knew that if I had made a diagnosis of acute abdomen which required surgery I was unlikely to be wrong and that even if he came to see the patient he wouldn't arrive at a different conclusion. He told me to ring Mr Jones again and tell him that Mr Humphrey had full confidence in the clinical judgement of his Registrar with whom he had worked for almost two years. He also told me to do the operation with or without the Gynaecologists.

"Just get on with it. Do an up and down incision," he said.

I rang Mr Jones and explained to him the conversation I just had with Mr Humphrey.

He said in no uncertain terms, "If your Consultant has confidence in you, you do the operation. I am not coming."

We were back to square one again.

The SHO in A&E who was a witness to this saga said, "This is what happens when an ambulance brings a patient here who should have been taken to the other place."

I told him that the ambulance crew were not to be blamed. They brought the woman to the nearest A&E to avoid any delay in her care and had to be commended for their decision. I suppose the Consultants concerned were not to be blamed either. Mr Jones had never seen me or worked with me. He couldn't be sure that I was not trying to sell him a dummy, trying to send a Surgical case to the Gynaecologist. Mr Humphrey knew me and had worked with me. He knew that I was not a 'trigger happy' Registrar who would consider feasibility an excuse for surgery. He was confident that this lady needed an operation if I thought it was necessary and sending her across to the other hospital was not advisable. This was not the time or the occasion to play the blame game.

I decided that we would get the patient to theatre as soon as we could. The house officer had already sent blood samples to the laboratory and blood was cross matched and ready for transfusion. I went and had a word with the theatre sister who allowed me to do the operation ahead of the Orthopaedic case which was already booked. I telephoned the Orthopaedic Registrar who was very understanding; he did not object. The Anaesthetist was also very helpful and the patient was on the operation table with in a short while.

I would have liked to do a small 'bikini' incision across the lower abdomen but my boss Mr Humphrey had asked me to do an up and down incision. This was because in case it was not a ruptured ectopic pregnancy, there was the sufficient access to do whatever other operation was required to be done.

"Typical of the General Surgeon," I said to myself.

Mr Humphrey was about to retire in a few months' time. He was an excellent Surgeon. Calm, cool and methodical, he was capable of doing complex and difficult operations successfully and he had enough experience to draw from, having worked as a Consultant Surgeon for almost thirty-three years. I had always admired him and the unhurried and skilful way in which he did surgical procedures. On this occasion I was a bit disappointed that I couldn't do a transverse incision but I decided to follow his instruction and to do a small 'up and down' incision, just below the umbilicus. (Her bikini might still be able to cover the scar!)

The House Officer in Surgery, who was normally very busy in the wards looking after inpatients and sorting out elective and emergency admissions, decided to come to theatre and assist me because there was no SHO in Surgery in that hospital. As soon as I opened the peritoneum, the thin sac enveloping the abdominal contents, blood gushed out. The young woman had a distended abdomen simply because the ectopic pregnancy she had in her right Fallopian tube had ruptured and blood and fluid had accumulated inside, as I had suspected.

What had happened in the private clinic in Cardiff is a mystery. Did she really have products of conception removed by D&C? In that case she had twin pregnancy, one foetus lodged in the uterus and the other on the right Fallopian tube. In any case, I removed the ruptured right tube and ovary, carried out a peritoneal lavage and closed the abdomen with a vacuum drain in place. She was given appropriate antibiotic prophylaxis as well.

The twenty-two year old woman whom the ambulance took to the nearest rather than the 'correct' hospital, spent five days in the surgical ward in the main hospital and was allowed home after an uneventful recovery. An outpatient appointment with Mr Jones, the Gynaecologist, was requested.

Thankfully Surgery and Gynaecology are under the same roof at present in that particular hospital. Moves are afoot to close the Gynaecology and Obstetrics Department in the General Hospital twenty-five miles away when patients in similar predicament will have a twenty-five mile journey to get the appropriate attention.

THE CHILD WHO HAD APPENDICITIS

It was about thirty-three years ago. I was working as a Surgical Senior House Officer in a hospital in the North of England. The contract was for one year, during six months of which there was no cover from the Surgical Registrar. That was because there was only one Registrar for four Consultant Surgeons. There were four SHOs and two of whom only were covered by him for the first six months and the other two scheduled to be covered during the next six months. In other words, the SHOs had to act up as Registrars with only the Consultant above them, to deal with emergency cases, for six months during their one year contract. The Consultants therefore appointed only experienced and trustworthy junior doctors as their SHOs.

I had already worked in the same unit as a Pre-Registration House Officer for six months and the Consultant Surgeon Mr Kirkwood was pleased with me. He appointed me as his SHO after a tough interview process in spite of four other strong candidates. I had not passed the FRCS (Fellowship of the Royal College of Surgeons) examination but he always addressed me as 'Mr Jay'. He never called me by my first name. He had already retired when he was sixty-five and was doing a very long locum in this hospital. He lived twenty-five miles away and obviously depended on his SHO for the management of the emergency cases. He always made sure that the day after he was on call, he would do a detailed ward rounds to see what were the cases admitted and how well they were handled.

One day Mr Kirkwood had finished his theatre list and he was about to go home when the Consultant in Paediatrics telephoned and asked him if he would see a child in the Paediatric unit and rule out appendicitis. He asked me if I would go and see the child and he went home.

The child was only four years old. He was not at all cooperative. Even though I had warmed up my hand on the radiator before touching his abdomen he was resentful and fidgety. He was holding his abdomen tight during his attempts to remove my hand from his tummy. I didn't have a satisfactory examination of the child. He didn't look unwell and was playful and cheerful when I was not trying to examine him.

I told the staff nurses in the ward and the parents of the child that I would come back when he was a bit more settled and examine him again. Unfortunately, it so happened that during the rest of the evening I was so busy that I didn't have the chance to see the child again till late in the night. When I came back to the ward at 10 p.m. I was told that the child was peacefully asleep. I decided to leave him alone and see him again during the ward rounds in the morning.

In the morning when Mr Kirkwood came for his ward-rounds the first thing he asked me was, "Did that child have appendicitis?" I explained to him what had happened. He said, "Let us begin the rounds in the Paediatric ward."

We walked down the stairs to the paediatric unit. Mr Kirkwood examined the now more relaxed child, sitting beside him, and when he finished the examination he looked up at me, as if asking me why an operation was not done the previous night. He stood up and said to me, "Examine him now and tell me what you think."

The child didn't hold his tummy tight or try to push away my hand. He was more at ease than before. I found that he had guarding, localised tenderness in the area of the appendix and rebound tenderness suggestive of acute appendicitis. I felt sad and guilty that I had not diagnosed it the previous night. I also felt that I let Mr Kirkwood down. We asked the staff to prepare the child for theatre and instructed the House Officer to obtain the consent from parents, book the theatre and inform the anaesthetist.

After the ward rounds I went and did the operation to remove the child's appendix. The appendix was inflamed. I was relieved that it was not perforated. The child made an excellent recovery and was allowed home after three days.

I had learned a valuable lesson that day. Whatever the excuse, postponing a decision may rob you of valuable time. When I was a young boy keen to postpone my homework for another day my father used to tell me that 'procrastination is the thief of time'. How very true!

THE GIRL WHO DIDN'T HAVE APPENDICITIS

The Paediatric Senior House officer (SHO) at the children's hospital telephoned me. "Could you please come and see a twelve-year-old girl. We think she has acute appendicitis."

I was the Surgical Registrar on call based in the main hospital three miles away. As soon as I had finished what I was doing in the operation theatre, I went over to see the child. Before I left, I had warned the theatre staff that if I decided to do an operation they would have to come over there and open the theatre at the paediatric hospital so that I could do the operation on the child. That was the existing arrangement for emergency paediatric surgery.

The girl was not a big twelve-year-old. She was thin and she looked ten rather than twelve years of age. Her father was with her; the mother was not. I was told there were other younger siblings to look after and that was why she couldn't come. The history was not typical of appendicitis. She was not unwell until she developed abdominal pain in the morning that day. It was not central abdominal pain shifting to the right side as in most cases of appendicitis. However, the story (clinical history) from a child cannot always be absolutely depended on. She may be influenced by the intimidating atmosphere of a hospital, presence of several doctors and nurses and other children often screaming or in distress in the background.

Examining her I had no doubt that she had localised peritonitis in the area of appendix, in the right lower abdomen. I told her father and the paediatric team that she had to get her appendix removed. The father's consent for the operation was obtained. The child had been kept starving already, anticipating this possibility.

I telephoned the theatre team and the Anaesthetist on call to come over to the children's hospital. Within an hour the child was on the table anaesthetised and ready.

Unfortunately I had to do the operation without a junior doctor in Surgery to assist me. The consultants were lucky that they always had a Registrar assisting them to do operations in elective operation lists as well as emergency operations. We, the Registrars, were handicapped because there was no Senior House Officer (SHO) in surgery in that hospital. The nursing staff were exemplary! Bless them! They were very helpful and always trying to assist as well as they could. But they were mainly concerned about keeping count of the swabs and instruments which was their main responsibility.

I placed a small transverse incision in the right lower abdomen in the area of the appendix. When I opened the peritoneum, to my surprise, the appendix looked normal. However, there was dirty and almost purulent fluid in the abdomen. My clinical impression of 'peritonitis' was correct but where was the source of the problem? There was no evidence of an inflamed Meckel's diverticulum (an abnormality of the small intestine, the inflammation of which resembles appendicitis) or any other visible abnormality. There was no mesenteric adenitis (inflammation of the lymph glands in the mesentery, the flat frill of the intestines.) either.

I decided that a laparotomy (full surgical exploration of abdomen) was necessary and that I should inform the Consultant Surgeon on call at this stage. I telephoned him from the theatre.

It was Mr Knight. He said he would come and give me a hand. Within half an hour he arrived. He took over from me and did a separate small upper abdominal mid line incision. Soon we found that it was a perforated duodenal ulcer! It was most unusual that a girl of twelve had a burst peptic ulcer! The ulcer was patched up with omentum (the frill on the stomach) sutured over it. The abdomen was washed out with saline, antibiotics commenced and the wound closed with absorbable sutures and a small vacuum drain in place.

When we went to the ward and told the girl's father that it was not appendicitis and that it was an ulcer which was perforated he said, "Oh! I had an operation for perforated ulcer when I was fourteen years old."

Without any hesitation he pulled up his shirt and showed us the scar for proof!

Did the child suffer from a familial condition? We, Surgeons, left that question to the clever Paediatricians to investigate. I had to rush back to the main hospital where emergency cases were waiting to be seen by the Surgical Registrar on call.

THE ONE WHO FLED FROM HIS BED

The last case on the routine operation list that afternoon was a right hemi-colectomy, an operation to remove a malignant tumour on the large bowel. The Consultant Surgeon had left the theatre early asking me to do the case. Everything went well. When the abdomen was being closed with sutures the Senior House Officer in Surgery (SHO) assisting me said that he had booked an emergency case, an 'exploration of a testis'. I was the registrar on call that day and night. He said, "I could send for the patient to be brought to theatre if you would like and we could get it over with because there were no other case booked in theatre on the emergency list."

Usually the Orthopaedic trauma cases were endlessly waiting for emergency theatre slots as were the Gynaecological cases or Caesarean Sections. Obviously it was best to get emergency cases done when there was a lull in theatre activity. In those days there was no separate theatre room or anaesthetist to do CEPOD (emergency) lists as there are in most hospitals nowadays. CEPOD lists were established after a Confidential Enquiry into peri-operative Deaths(CEPOD) uncovered convincing data of increased peri-operative mortality when operations were done late at night and in the early hours of the morning. Normally, emergencies had to wait till the elective cases were all finished and the theatre staff, theatre rooms and anaesthetists were available.

I asked the SHO, Mark, what the exploration was all about. "Is it a suspected torsion of testis?"

"No," he replied. "It was a man unloading bricks from a lorry when he got hit in the scrotum by a falling brick. The weight of the brick hitting his private parts had apparently pushed the right testis into the groin and it had to be explored and brought down."

Mark was on call with me that night. He was a fairly experienced SHO and was very keen to get as many operations on his log book as possible. He said he was happy to do the case himself if I wanted to go and grab some dinner in the hospital canteen.

I told him, "I am not convinced by this story of a falling brick pushing a testis up into the groin." I asked Mark if he had seen the patient. He said he had not. The Surgical House Officer had seen the patient and admitted him to the emergency Surgical Admissions Unit. The Consultant Surgeon on call, Mr Parker, had apparently done evening rounds and agreed with the plan for the exploration.

I told Mark that I wanted to go and see the patient myself before bringing him down to theatre. When we finished the case we were doing, both of us made our way to the Surgical Admissions Unit.

There we saw a twenty-five year old man all prepared, gowned and ready for theatre. He had painkilling injection of morphine given intravenously because he was groaning with pain. He also had a drip running because he had been starved for a few hours.

I told the Ward Sister that I wanted to examine the man. The curtains were drawn around him when I looked at his groin, Mark by my side. I was surprised that there was no visible bruise on his groin or scrotum. True, I couldn't feel his right testis in the groin or the right hemi-scrotum. However, there was no visible sign of a recent injury. There was no visible scar of a previous operation either. He could have had an undescended testis which was still in the abdomen. I couldn't see the point of doing an emergency operation looking for an absent or intra-abdominal testis. The whole case was bizarre and the credibility of the patient's story dubious.

I asked the Ward Sister if Mr Parker, the Consultant, had examined the patient. She said she was not sure. I told her that I was not doing an operation on this man that evening and that I would speak to the Consultant. I instructed the sister not to give him any more pain relief injections.

"Let us go to the canteen and get something to eat before any genuine emergency comes in," I said to Mark and we went downstairs.

When we finished our meal I telephoned Mr Parker. He had not examined the patient. When I described my examination findings and told him my view that there was no indication for an emergency operation he agreed with me without any reservation. He asked me to tell Mark to get a camera and go to the patient and take his photo, telling him that he was an interesting case. As it happened Mark had an excellent Nikon camera with which he was taking photos during the doctors' party the other day. He said he would go and take a photo.

I decided to go and read the newspapers in the doctors' sitting room. It was a quiet day so far but later on it may turn out to be terribly busy. After about half an hour Mark came to see me, laughing all the way. He said that as soon as he saw the camera, the patient pulled out the cannula and drip from his arm and got dressed quickly and ran away. He was there for the morphine and he had got what he wanted. He didn't want his photo placed in other A/E units of neighbouring hospitals to alert them to watch out for him. What he told the nurses about his address was true: 'no fixed abode!'

THE MAN WHO DID NOT HAVE A HEART ATTACK

About thirty years ago, one of the towns in England where I worked had three different hospitals, three miles apart, for medical, surgical and gynaecological emergency admissions. I worked as a Surgical Registrar there and was based in the main hospital where all surgical emergencies were brought. Children and general medical emergencies were taken to the children's hospital and the medical admissions unit three miles away from where I was working. However I used to get called, not infrequently, to both the children's hospital and the medical wards to see patients and rule out surgical conditions which needed to be seen urgently. One day I was asked to see a patient in the cardiac unit in the hospital three miles away. The Medical Registrar who spoke to me explained.

"A seventy-two year old man was admitted the previous night with severe central chest pain of sudden onset. It was thought to be a heart attack and was treated as such. But the ECG (Electro cardiogram) was normal, except for a slow heart rate of fifty, and other investigations were normal. Now we wonder if it is something surgical. Could you please come and see him?"

Some of the cardiac enzymes and the advanced investigations done routinely to diagnose a heart attack these days were unavailable back then, at that time.

The medical team looking after him noticed that his abdomen was slightly distended. The patient had a low blood pressure but as I mentioned earlier his pulse rate was not fast. Ultra sound scans, CT scans and MRI scans were not available in that hospital thirty years ago.

The Physicians, having ruled out a cardiac event after observing him overnight eventually wondered, "Is this an atypical presentation of a surgical condition?"

His abdominal distension was getting gradually bigger and he was complaining of abdominal pain as well as chest pain. Repeated blood tests showed that he was becoming anaemic. They wondered if he had some bleeding inside the abdomen, say from a slowly leaking aortic aneurysm. (An aneurysm is a ballooning of the blood vessel usually the aorta, the big arterial tube carrying blood from the heart to the abdomen and the lower limbs). That was why I was asked to see the patient and rule out a surgical condition.

The possibility of a leaking aneurysm will alert any Surgical Registrar on call for emergencies. I arrived in the cardiac unit swiftly, leaving behind any non-essential emergencies to be dealt with later.

The man was all wired up, still attached to various monitors and leads. He was pleasant and cooperative in spite of his predicament. He said that the whole problem was of sudden onset the previous night. Even though he said that the pain was initially in the central area of the chest, he admitted that he couldn't be sure that there was no abdominal pain at that time. He did not have any significant past medical or surgical history except for mildly elevated blood pressure for which he was on medication. He was a retired shop keeper who with his gay partner had left London where they were in business together for over forty years. He admitted that he used to have more than average alcohol consumption in the past and that he had cut down drastically since his retirement.

On examining him I was convinced that there was an intra-abdominal problem. He had a distended abdomen and signs of peritonitis. He looked pale. There were clinical signs of free fluid in the abdomen. One baffling observation was that his pulse rate was still only around fifty. Fast pulse rate is normally the result when patients bleed and go into shock unless they are on certain tablets like beta blockers or they are very athletic individuals. It was because of the slow pulse rate and the central chest pain that he was admitted to the cardiac unit suspected of a heart attack. Having ruled out a heart attack, the physicians wondered about the possibility of a leaking aortic aneurysm, not without justification. I considered that possibility but was surprised that he did not have any back ache at all. Patients with leaking aortic aneurysms usually have severe back ache as a symptom when they present themselves. The fact that he looked too well to have had a leaking aneurysm from the previous evening onwards was also perplexing.

The only way to have an answer was to do a laparotomy. I decided that he had to be moved to the surgical ward in the main hospital and prepared for surgery. The Cardiology Consultant reassured me that there was no compromising cardiac condition and that he was fit enough to be transferred three miles away for surgery.

It was time for me to speak to the Consultant Surgeon on call, Mr Murphy. He was a very experienced surgeon who was about to retire after about forty years of service to the NHS. I had always admired the cool, methodical and competent way he carried out surgical procedures. I was convinced that his presence in theatre was necessary in this case and it would be foolish of me to try and do the case on my own. I explained the case carefully to Mr Murphy and told him that I would arrange the theatre and ensure that there would be enough blood available for transfusion.

Thankfully, the transfer to the main hospital three miles away in an ambulance did not make the man any worse. The junior doctors in the cardiac unit had already acted on my request and several units of blood were made available for transfusion by the time he was wheeled to the theatre. His gay partner insisted on travelling with him in the ambulance. He was a very concerned man and he walked with the patient, who was in the trolley being wheeled into theatre, holding his hands up to the anaesthetic room.

After examining the patient in the theatre, Mr Murphy said he was also wondering what we would find when we do the laparotomy. The slow pulse rate, the absence of back ache, the presentation with sudden severe central chest pain; all these were challenging and rather confusing signs and symptoms to arrive at a definite pre-operative diagnosis.

The transfusion was well in progress when the abdomen was opened through a mid-line incision. As was suspected, there was evidence of considerable intra-abdominal bleeding. Initially we were not sure where it was bleeding from. It was not an aortic aneurysm. The aorta looked normal. When all the accumulated blood and debris was sucked away with the vacuum device, it was found that the bleeding was from the left lobe of the liver. The man had a tumour there which had ruptured spontaneously. No wonder that the abdomen was distended up with blood, reactive peritoneal fluid and necrotic tissue from the ruptured large tumour of the liver. There was also evidence of cirrhosis of liver from his chronic alcohol abuse.

Calm and collected as always, Mr Murphy took over the operation from me and carefully removed the left lobe of the liver in its entirety. (Fortunately it was the left lobe of the liver which was involved and a complete resection of it was possible.) He stopped all bleeding with ligatures and diathermy, did a peritoneal lavage, inserted a vacuum drain and left me to close the abdomen. Before he left the theatre, impressed with the way he did the procedure, I asked him, "Have you ever done this operation before?"

He smiled and said, "No," and walked way. Later on, one day when we were alone in the doctors' room of the operation theatre, waiting for the next case on the list to be anaesthetised, he emphasised the importance of keeping one's cool even in situations of uncertainty and having the courage of conviction to go ahead and do a procedure which you think is necessary to save a patient's life.

The patient had a critical post-operative period. He was jaundiced and quite unwell recovering from his nasty ordeal. His gay partner, a man probably of the same age, was by his bedside whenever he was allowed to be there. Up to that time I had never seen a gay man so committed to his partner. Mind you, I had not seen many gay people and in those days people were reluctant to openly admit that they were gay.

After keeping him in the intensive care unit for two days he was moved to the general surgical ward. The patient made a remarkable recovery and after two weeks and was allowed home.

THE MAN WITH THE REDUCIBLE HERNIA

When I worked as a Senior House Officer (SHO) in Orthopaedics in one of the hospitals in England, the contract was for one year, six months of which was in a satellite hospital where I had the responsibility to clerk and admit some urological patients for routine operations there. My special interest was Urology, not Orthopaedics and I loved that posting and the experience I got there.

One day when I was clerking patients for the next day's Urology operations, I came across a man who was on the operation list for 'repair of right hydrocele'. (A hydrocele is a collection of fluid in the scrotal sac). He was a taxi driver and he asked me when he would be allowed to get back home and to his work.

"Being a self-employed man, any time lost is money lost," he reminded me.

I told him that he would normally be home the next day. In those days that was the practice even though nowadays in most hospitals it will be a day case procedure.

When I examined him I found that he had a large swelling involving the right groin and the scrotum and that it was in fact a hernia rather than a hydrocele. I looked at the notes and found that it was the Consultant who had seen the man in the clinic. I examined the patient again and confirmed that the swelling was completely reducible back into the abdomen with gentle pressure and persuasion, confirming that it was a hernia.

I told the man, "This is a hernia. The wound after the operation would be in the right groin, not the scrotum."

Doing an incision in the scrotum, assuming it to be a hydrocele, carried the risk of cutting straight into the bowel in the hernia, which had come down into the scrotal sac.

When I finished clerking all the patients I approached the Ward Sister and told her my finding and my concern that the patient would have the risk of an incision on his scrotum if the diagnosis was not corrected in the case notes and the theatre list.

She said, "Mr Clive Lloyd, the Urology consultant, would normally come in the evening to see the patients admitted for the next day, even though the operation list was going to be done by a Clinical Assistant Mr Patel, who happened to be a local GP. I will certainly convey your message to Mr Lloyd."

When Mr Lloyd came to the ward as was expected, I was not there. The Ward Sister told him about what I had said after my examination of the patient. She showed him what I had written when I clerked the patient. However he was not prepared to change his mind and admit that he was wrong and I, a mere SHO, was right! I am not sure if he examined the patient again. If he did, it was done only half-heartedly. He told the sister that it was a hydrocele. He did not make any alteration in the theatre list.

The Surgical Registrar, a handsome man with a double barrelled name, at the sight of whom all the young nurses were excited and cheerful, came to the ward after his outpatient clinic was finished. I told him about the man with the large hernia posted for 'hydrocele' surgery. He was a very pleasant guy who had just passed his FRCS examination. He was keen to examine the patient himself. After a few minutes he came and told me,

"I agree with you. It is a hernia. I just reduced it and it went back in to the abdomen when gentle pressure was applied. The scrotal swelling completely disappeared. It is not a Hydrocele."

The next day when the Clinical Assistant came to do the operation he came to the ward first. I explained to him the situation. He said that he would examine the patient and get the appropriate consent.

The patient had a groin incision because Mr Patel, the would-be Surgeon, examined the patient and confirmed that it was in fact a large hernia. Unfortunately the poor patient had a post-operative wound infection which delayed his departure from the ward. He was not pleased because he could not get back to work as early as he hoped.

To this day I don't know why Mr Lloyd, a decent man and very capable Urologist, who worked in a famous teaching hospital as well the District General Hospital where I worked, did not arrive at the correct diagnosis and change the operation list. May be he knew that Mr Patel, the Clinical Assistant, could be entrusted to examine the patient before doing the operation and to place the incision in the appropriate place. May be his ego simply swallowed up his better judgement.

THE LADY WHO HAD GALLSTONE ILEUS

One day when I was the on call Surgical Registrar there was an emergency admission of a fifty-eight year old lady, Judith Sanders, who had intestinal obstruction. The presentation was with clear cut signs and symptoms. She had a very distended abdomen. She was vomiting intermittently and she said that she also had colicky abdominal pain. The abdominal X-ray, which the House Officer had already arranged, suggested small bowel obstruction.

Only when I saw her did I realise that Judith was also an Achondroplasiac (born with a short stature, short trunk, hands and legs). She was obviously unwell but very cooperative.

I asked her, "Have you had any constipation or diarrhoea previously?"

She replied, "No. Never. I have had some indigestion from time to time. I always dealt with that myself, taking some Gaviscone prescribed by my GP or some Rennies which I could get over the counter." Her symptoms were of a short duration of less than twenty-four hours. She said that she never had an operation in the past.

I explained to the lady, "The X-ray suggests an obstruction of the small bowel. We have to do an operation to sort out whatever the problem causing the bowel obstruction is."

She was also told about the probability of a colostomy bag, in case she had a large bowel pathology causing the obstruction, even though every effort would be made to avoid it. It is important to keep the patient fully informed and getting the informed consent before proceeding to administer general anaesthesia. She was tolerant and compliant when a tube had to be inserted through the nose into her stomach for suction of the accumulated fluid, air and other stomach contents.

Normally the Consultant Surgeon on call would not expect to be informed of every operation the Registrar was going to do. Over a period of time there develops an understanding and trust between the Consultant and the Registrar. Of course, any complicated cases which the Registrar himself finds challenging will be discussed with the Consultant. This arrangement has probably changed over the years and I suspect that now most Consultant Surgeons would expect Registrars to tell them about any operation they were planning to do.

The House Officer was not too busy that day. Normally, he had to clerk all the patients for the next day's elective operation lists, take all the emergency calls from GPs and look after the sick patients in the ward, leaving him little time to do anything else. (Nowadays, pre-assessment clinics run by nurses do clerking and pre-operative blood test, ECGs, etc. for patients to be admitted on elective operation lists.) He said he would come to the theatre and assist me in the case. I was pleased because doing a laparotomy with the scrub nurse assisting you is not ideal. Even though the nurses are extremely obliging and cooperative they have their main responsibility to make sure that the swabs count has to be correct and that the instruments are all accounted for.

On the operation table Judith occupied only about half of its length. When the Anaesthetist gave me the nod to go ahead, I did a mid-line incision and opened the abdomen. Instantly loops and loops of distended small bowel escaped outside. I carefully inspected the bowel to look for the site of obstruction. To my surprise, I found that a stone, about three centimetres in size, was obstructing the small bowel at its junction with the large bowel (the ileo-caecal junction). It had eroded through the wall of the gall bladder and the adjoining small bowel and travelled down to the site of obstruction.

Even though I had read about the condition of gall stone ileus in surgical text books, it was the first time I ever saw a case presenting as emergency. I removed the stone through a small incision on the bowel wall and sutured the wound with vicryl absorbable sutures.

The gross distension of the bowel was already deflated. The loops of bowel which came out were returned to the abdomen and the abdominal wound was closed with a vacuum drain in place. The appropriate antibiotic prophylaxis was already given and the patient was sent back to the ward.

Late that evening, before going to bed I decided to go and have a look at the lady. To my horror, I found that she was in severe respiratory distress. The night nurse in charge of the ward said, "I was going to bleep the House Officer to come and see this lady. She started to breathe abnormally only a few minutes ago."

I borrowed the stethoscope from the House Officer who was with me and listened to her chest. She had pulmonary oedema (fluid in her lungs). Immediately I gave her a dose of Frusemide, a diuretic, intravenously to get rid of the fluid from the lungs. As we waited anxiously by her bedside, gradually she became better and better and eventually back to normal. The problem was caused by her fluid regime of three litres of normal saline over twenty-four hours and the rapidity with which the drip was going. It was my fault that I did not write the regime myself after I had finished writing the operation notes. For a lady of her short stature and low body weight, three litres of fluid over twenty-four hours was too much and the last one litre of fluid was going too fast and would have finished in three hours rather than eight. No wonder her lungs were overloaded with fluid and couldn't function properly!

Thereafter, her post-operative recovery was slow but steady and she was discharged home after ten days.

THE LADY WHO HAD OVARIAN TORSION

When I was working as a Senior House Officer (SHO) in Surgery in Manchester I had six months in a one year contract when I had to shoulder responsibilities of a Registrar as well. That was because there was only one Registrar for four Consultant Surgeons and he could cover only two of the four SHOs. Whenever I was on call, I made it a point to sleep in the on call room in the hospital building so that the Pre-Registration House officer was not alone to look after patients.

Towards the end of my two-year posting I had taken two weeks' leave because my wife was pregnant and her due date was imminent. The leave was to begin on a Monday but I was on call that week end including Sunday.

Sunday evening my wife telephoned me and asked, "Could you sleep here at home tonight rather than the duty room because I have been getting some nagging pains in my lower abdomen."

I spoke to the House Officer on call with me and he promised me that he would be extra vigilant. "Go home. In case there is any need I will bleep you immediately," he said.

The House Officer, Dr Jim Ryan, was a fairly experienced man himself, having worked in South Africa before he came to England. He was fed up with the apartheid system and the atrocities happening there and had come to the UK for higher studies and possibly permanent residence here. He was a very loyal colleague and keen to help me whenever he could.

It was fairly quiet that evening compared to other 'on call' evenings. There were no cases waiting to go to theatre. I went around the ward with Dr Ryan and made sure that there was no issues waiting to be sorted out. Eventually I decided to go home and see my wife and sleep there during the night, for the first time in two years, on a night when on call.

At about ten at night Dr Ryan bleeped me and told me about a young woman of twenty-five years whom he had just admitted.

"The GP sent her in as a case of suspected appendicitis but I don't think she has appendicitis," he said. "I don't think anything is seriously wrong with her. By tomorrow morning she will be able to go home," he added. He sounded rather emphatic and I thought there was no need to go and see her then and there. Before I hang up he asked me, "Is it all right if I gave her some Pethidine?"

Immediately my antennae of caution were up. I asked him, "If you think that the woman is all right, why give Pethidine?"

Then Dr Ryan said, "Oh she is saying that she is in a lot of pain though I am not convinced."

May be my colleague, in his eagerness to help me, was inadvertently belittling the symptoms of this lady. I decided that it was high time I went and saw this lady myself. I made my way to the hospital.

The woman was a quite sensible one and gave me a very good history of her illness. Dr Ryan was quite right. The pain was of sudden onset and severe. It was not characteristic of appendicitis. Acute appendicitis usually presents as a gradual pain first felt in the umbilical area and then shifting towards the right lower abdomen in most people, even though there can be exceptions. I could also see why she deserved some strong pain relief. She was in severe pain. When I examined her I found that her pain was confined to the right lower abdomen. I suspected that she had an ovarian torsion (twisting of the ovary and tube or twisting of a large cyst of the ovary) rather than a surgical condition because of her convincing story of sudden onset of the pain and the localised nature of the pain.

I bleeped the on call Registrar for Gynaecology, Mr Chuku Emeka. He was a very pleasant Nigerian gentleman who had passed the FRCS as well as the MRCOG, i.e. he had higher qualifications in Surgery as well as Gynaecology. He came to see the woman shortly afterwards.

After examining her he told me, "You are probably right. Why don't you also come to the theatre so that we can do the operation together, in case it is anything surgical."

I agreed.

The necessary pre-operative preparations were all done and the patient was in theatre by 11.30 p.m. Mr Emeka did the operation and I assisted him. It was the torsion of a large cyst of the ovary. Thankfully, it was not the ovary itself and it was easily spared and the cyst excised. The patient was taken over to the Gynaecology ward from the theatre.

It was around 1.30 a.m. when I got back to my on call room. I decided not to go back home and disturb my wife and six-year-old daughter. I went to sleep.

By 2.30 a.m. my wife got the switch board to bleep me.

"You better come now. I am getting frequent contractions."

She was a doctor herself and knew what she was talking about. I woke up Dr Khan, my colleague who was the SHO of another Surgical Unit. He was peacefully sleeping at his home. I apologised and asked him to cover me till morning. From the morning onwards I was on leave any way. After arranging my cover I rushed back home. My wife was in full labour pain. I asked for the ambulance and informed the maternity ward.

The ambulance arrived promptly and within three hours of my wife being admitted to the maternity ward, my second daughter arrived promptly too. It was an eventful night.

THE LADY WHO DECLINED SURGERY

Mrs Janet Smith was a fifty-year-old widow who had recurrent cholecystitis (inflammation of the gall bladder). She was rather chubby but not too fat. She was not the so called typical 'fatty, fertile, female of forty' who is said to develop gall bladder disease. She hated hospitals and often didn't attend her outpatient appointments. Mr Griffiths, the Consultant Surgeon looking after her was often frustrated that this lady was ignoring his advice to have surgery to remove the gall bladder and that she was also becoming a habitual non-attender in the clinics.

One day Mrs Smith was admitted as an emergency with severe colicky pain in her tummy. She was found to be jaundiced. In view of her previous history of cholecystitis she was thought to have obstructive jaundice as a result of a stone moving from the gall bladder to the common bile duct and causing obstruction to the flow of bile in to the intestine. This provisional diagnosis was proven to be correct when a special X-ray (cholecystogram) was done. It showed stones in the bile duct which explained why she was getting severe colicky abdominal pain and why she had jaundice.

The next day when Mr Griffiths came for his routine ward rounds he found Mrs Smith in the ward, visibly yellow and unwell. He said, "I had warned you that this was a risk you were taking when you refused surgery previously."

She was sad but unapologetic. "Mr Griffiths, you know I have my reasons."

The Surgeon agreed that he was aware of her concerns but told her, "This time I have little room for manoeuvre. This is an emergency and we have to remove the gall stones from the bile duct for bile to flow freely into the intestine. Otherwise it can be life threatening."

"All right, will you do the operation yourself?" she asked.

"Yes," he answered emphatically, without hesitation. "We will wait till you are a bit better and your temperature has come down. By the time of my next operation list in a few days, you will be ready for theatre."

Still sceptical, she asked him if there were any tablets he could take to dissolve the stones. He said there were none.

"In some centres they are using a telescope placed in the stomach and approach the bile duct through the intestine but that also involves putting you to sleep and the success rate for the procedure is not great because people are only trying the method out."

The lady said she would consent to undergo the operation.

In the theatre I was assisting Mr Griffiths when he operated on Mrs

Smith. It was a very difficult undertaking for even Mr Griffiths, a man with about thirty years' experience as a Consultant Surgeon. He struggled because it was difficult to get at the stoned jammed in the common bile duct. After making a small incision into the bile duct he had to introduce a grabbing forceps and blindly feel for the stones further down in the lower end of the bile duct. There was no flexible telescope (choledochoscope) available those days to inspect and see the stones and grab them.

Eventually he removed all the stones he could feel with the instrument and removed the gall bladder. He stopped all bleeding and inserted a drainage T-tube in the bile duct which is normal procedure to ensure healing of the wound in the bile duct and the drainage of bile into intestine.

During the operation, Mr Griffiths confided in me the reason this lady had previously adamantly refused surgery. She had a dream one night that she had surgery to remove her gall bladder and that she died following the procedure. In one of the consultations she had told him about this dream and he had told her that dreams are just a reflection of the fear people have in their sub-conscious mind and that should not put her off. Now that the lady had come in as an emergency and the operation itself was rather hazardous the Surgeon told me that he hoped her dream would remain just a dream.

Mrs Smith had a tumultuous post-operative period. She developed acute pancreatitis (inflammation of the pancreas) which was a recognised complication of exploring the common bile duct and removing gall stones. Even the simple presence of stones in the bile duct can sometimes cause pancreatitis. She became very ill and gradually deteriorated. She was moved to the intensive care unit where the physicians and anaesthetists tried their level best. Eventually she succumbed to 'multiple systems failure' which meant that she developed liver, kidneys and lungs failure. After ten days in the ICU Mrs Smith passed away.

It was a very sad day for the surgical team. If only she had an operation earlier when MrGriffiths had suggested, the gall bladder could have been removed when the stones were still in it (and not moved into the common bile duct) and the fatal pancreatitis could have been perhaps avoided.

I remembered the famous play *Julius Caesar* and the dream Caeser's wife had in which she saw her husband being stabbed to death. That was Shakespearean fiction. This was a real life incident in which a fear the patient had harboured in her sub conscious mind unfortunately came to pass.

THE BOY WHO WAS THROWN OUT OF THE WIND SCREEN

The accident happened when their Volvo saloon car had to be stopped suddenly to avoid hitting a careless pedestrian who crossed the road without looking to his right. The Vauxhall Astra coming directly behind was travelling over forty miles in a thirty-mile-an-hour zone and could not stop in time to avoid a collision. The incident occurred at a time when seat belts were not compulsory. The impact of the collision was such that a three-year-old boy held by his mother in her lap was thrown out of the Volvo through the windscreen. Others in both cars had only minor injuries.

The ambulance and the police car were at the site of the accident without delay. The child and the shocked parents were rushed to the Accident and Emergency Department. The driver and passengers of the Vauxhall had no serious injuries and were allowed home when police had completed their formalities.

When the Senior House Officer in the Casualty Department asked me to see the three-year-old child and rule out a head injury, I went and saw the child. He was conscious and he had surprisingly few visible injuries apart from skin abrasions and a bump on the side of his head above the right ear.

The X-rays showed that he had not broken any limbs or ribs. Interpretation of a child skull X-ray can be tricky because the bones are not yet fully developed and bony joints can look like fractures. However, I had worked as an SHO and a Registrar in A/E Departments in the past before I was appointed as a Surgical Registrar and had the experience of reviewing numerous X-rays of skulls previously. I was concerned about a suspicious looking line on the temporal bone of the child's skull which looked very much like a fracture.

The parents said that the child cried immediately after the accident. They didn't think he lost consciousness. I noticed that he was drowsy and trying to sleep in between crying. I decided that the child should be sent to a centre where an immediate CT scan could be done to rule out a blood clot inside the skull.

The nearest available CT scan was in the neurology centre fifty miles away. I telephoned them and spoke to the Neurosurgery Registrar on call at length. He insisted that even though they had the facility to do a CT Scan they didn't have any children's unit and a child couldn't be accepted there in case neurological surgery was required. I tried my level best to appeal to his compassion but he insisted that he was helpless in this situation. He suggested that I tried Guy's Hospital in London. (Isn't it the standard technique to get rid of you from the phone line, giving you another number to ring?)

Without wasting valuable time, I telephoned Guy's Hospital. The Surgical Registrar there was a pleasant guy who re-directed me to another number and to try if there were beds available. Alas! There was absolutely no chance accepting a child because all children's beds were occupied.

For the next thirty-five minutes I sat there in the A/E ringing up various hospitals in London, *praying* that there will be somebody who will accept this child who was becoming drowsier and drowsier as time was going by. Honestly, I did pray. Whenever I was in a tight spot, as a Christian and a believer I have prayed for a favourable outcome for my patients. Thankfully, there is no legal restriction here in the UK, so far, against praying silently without anybody except God knowing about it!

King's College Hospital in London, at that time, was not attached to St Thomas' or Guy's Hospital, as is the case now. It was a separate Teaching Hospital before the re-organisation which bundled the three hospitals together. When I rang the on call Registrar there, I was simply clutching any available straw! To my surprise, when the man heard the story of this three-year-old child with probably a clot inside his skull and realised the urgency of the situation he told me to send the child in a 'blue light ambulance' and send him to King's College hospital straight away. I was delighted and I did precisely what I was asked to do. I arranged the ambulance straight away because I knew that there was no room for wishful thinking or complacency and that if my provisional diagnosis of a haemorrhage inside the skull was correct, any delay would be disastrous.

After the child and parents left, I had to go to theatre to do some emergency cases waiting to be done. Soon after, I was in the ward helping the House Officer. About four hours after the injured child left the A/E I had a telephone call from King's College Hospital London. It was the same Registrar with whom I had the conversation earlier.

"Hey buddy! The CT scan revealed an extra-dural haemorrhage which had caused a large clot in the skull pressing on the child's brain. We dealt with it immediately by evacuation through burr holes. Well done, in your efforts to send the child to safety."

I was immensely pleased and I thanked God that all ended well. I thanked the man for telephoning me and giving me a feed-back. It was a magnanimous gesture. Late in the evening I had a call from the A/E Sister saying that someone was there asking to speak to me. It was the father of the child. He just wanted to thank me in person.

I just told him, "Let us thank God that the child is safe."

THE HAND-OVER OF A POTENTIAL TIME BOMB

Handover of a surgical case could be very tricky, especially the Surgeon handing over the previous night's admission was a well-respected Senior Registrar. Maybe the patient came in the early hours of the morning and the on call SR had seen him after a very busy night when he made the decision to just observe him so that he could be discharged later on that day after the Consultant ward rounds. It was also safe practice to observe a patient and do an operation only if absolutely necessary.

When the Consultant Surgeon, Mr King came to do ward rounds he usually looked at the patients briefly and speedily because he had to get to the theatre to do his elective theatre list after finishing the rounds. When the nurse in charge of the ward told him that the patient was already seen by the Senior Registrar whose plan was to observe him and send him home later on the same day, he already had a pre-conceived idea that this patient was all right to go home. He examined the patient more speedily than the previous patient and agreed with the Senior Registrar. He walked on to the next patient.

Being the Registrar on call that day, I thought I should also examine the patient because he looked in some pain when Mr King left his bedside. I stayed back from the ward rounds crowd and enquired as to what the problem was.

The patient, Mr White, said, "I was all right till last evening when I went to bed. I woke up by in the middle of the night with a griping pain in my tummy which was coming and going in waves. I thought it was because I needed to open my bowels but nothing happened when I went to the toilet. In fact, I felt sick a couple of times. When the pain was not going away my wife called the ambulance and got me to casualty. The pain eased off when they gave me the injection. Now I think it is coming back again."

When I examined him I thought he was quite tender in the right side of the abdomen; it was localised tenderness and there was rebound tenderness. I wondered if it was an unusual presentation of appendicitis. People with kidney stones have pain coming in waves when the stone moves down the ureter (the natural tube connecting the kidney to the bladder) but they have pain radiating from the back to the front and don't usually have localised tenderness in the lower abdomen on examination.

I was convinced that Mr White could not be discharged home without a surgical exploration to rule out appendicitis.

I was in a difficult predicament. How can I go and tell a Consultant Surgeon, even though he was the junior most Consultant in the Department of Surgery, that I had a different opinion about a patient whom he had just examined in presence of the nurses and two House Officers? He had agreed with the opinion of the Senior Registrar and pronounced that the patient could go home later on. He would certainly feel belittled if a mere Registrar openly challenged his diagnosis in presence of his nurses and junior doctors. To offend a Consultant in such a situation could be equivalent to a career suicide.

Interestingly, one of the other Consultants in the Department of Surgery, Mr Bodkin, after examining a patient who was admitted as an emergency and handed over by another on call team, always would ask the patient if his Registrar could examine him as well.

He would say to the patient, "You see, these Registrars see emergencies all the time, much more often than I do. I value their opinion."

The patient would almost always agree, albeit reluctantly, to be examined by the Registrar accompanying the Consultant.

However, this was not Mr Bodkin.

I decided to wait till the ward rounds finished. It was a very prudent course of action. When the crowd dispersed and Mr King made his way to the theatre, I hurriedly caught up with him and walked with him. I said, "I am a bit concerned about Mr White. He is quite tender in the right lower abdomen and there is guarding on palpation. I think he ought to have an operation for a look at his appendix even though it is not a typical history of appendicitis." To exonerate the Senior Registrar I went on to say, "When the Senior Registrar examined him the patient already had an injection of Pethidine (an injection for pain relief) which may have masked the symptoms to some extent." I quite deliberately left Mr King out of the equation and made it look like a difference of opinion between me and the SR and placed the blame squarely on the pethidine injection.

"I am on call today and I am quite happy to do the procedure myself," I added.

Mr King suddenly became aware of the potential danger of a missed diagnosis. He put on his hat of caution. He knew that his examination of the man was far from thorough. He knew very well that sending home a patient who was in need of surgery, in spite of my warning, would not be wise. He told me, "Go ahead and have a look at his appendix but my hunch is that you won't find anything abnormal." He had to make clear that he supported the view of the SR not the concern of the Registrar.

I went back to the ward and explained to the Sister in charge that Mr King had a change of heart and that the patient should be prepared for theatre. The patient was pleased that something definitive was going to be done to find out more about his ailment and possibly cure it. His pain had returned with vehemence when the effect of the pain killing injection wore off. He gave consent for the operation without any hesitation.

At the time of surgery the Senior House Officer assisting me was quick to point out, *"Look, the appendix looks normal!"*

He also must have had his doubts before he came to theatre because the SR who saw the patient was a very popular and respected gentleman who was about to complete his long surgical training. There were rumours that he had already been unofficially offered a Consultant Surgeon's post in one of the hospitals in the Midlands.

True, the appendix looked entirely normal when we inspected it. I had opened the abdomen through an incision usually used to remove the appendix. If I were to have a detailed inspection of the other abdominal organs, I should do another incision or extend this further.

Convinced that his tenderness on clinical examination was localised in that area, I inspected the Caecum, the beginning of the large bowel. It was also normal. I wondered if he had an inflamed diverticulum of the small bowel called Meckel's diverticulum. There was no such diverticulum found.

However, I noticed a blue discolouration of the small bowel where I was looking for the diverticulum and wondered what had caused it. I was handling the bowel with care and had not caused any trauma. I also noticed that when I pulled up a little longer section of the discoloured area I felt some resistance. The loops of the small bowel wouldn't come up into my hand as easily as it was normally the case. Suddenly I realised that a section of the small bowel was stuck and trapped in the small recess behind the large bowel called the para colic fossa. The trapped section of the small bowel had its blood supply compromised. In other words, it was an internal strangulated hernia. That was why the patient had colicky abdominal pain and vomiting.

Internal hernias and the possibility of their strangulation are well-recognised and described in text books but they are very uncommon unless the patient had previous operations. Adhesions or small gaps in the mesentery created inadvertently by previous surgery could cause internal strangulations of intestines. This patient never had any previous surgery.

In my whole surgical career this was the only case I had seen of a spontaneously strangulated internal hernia. I gently widened the para colic 'hole', into which the loop of bowel had descended and got trapped, with scissors, and released the pressure on the strangulated bowel. The section of the small bowel that I pulled up easily thereafter was already blue but not overtly gangrenous. I used warm normal saline swabs again and again to bring circulation back to the bowel wall and managed it successfully. Otherwise I would have had to resect and remove the bowel devoid of blood supply and carry out anastomoses of the healthy ends. To prevent the same problem happening again, I closed the para colic gap using vicryl absorbable sutures.

I was relieved that the operation I carried out in spite of the reservations of my Consultant colleague was not in vain. I was more relieved that a vulnerable poor man whose life was in our hands was not let down by our indecision and that he did not come to any harm.

The Senior Registrar was on vacation for three weeks after this incident and I never had a chance to see him or talk to him about this case because my contract had finished by the time he returned. The Senior House Officer who assisted me had an opportunity to see the rare case of spontaneous internal strangulation of a loop of small bowel. The Consultant Surgeon Mr King, an excellent Surgeon who saved the lives of hundreds of patients before he retired from his illustrious career, did not speak to me about this case again. He must have read my operation notes and spoken to the SHO who assisted me. I did not want to talk to him about this either. Some people with bruised egos prefer to forget embarrassing episodes. The patient was discharged home in due course. He left the hospital, a happy man.

THE MAN WHO HAD A PERFORATED GULLET

I have come across a few rare emergency surgical cases in my career as a junior doctor. Often when I was on call I would see only routine cases like appendicitis, obstructed hernias, perforated peptic ulcers, intestinal obstructions, renal colic from kidney stones, soft tissue injuries and head injuries from accidents, burns and the like. However there have been some unusual cases also and I do remember them very well.

One day a sixty-five year old man who had very severe pain in his abdomen and chest was brought to the Accident and Emergency Department by ambulance. The Consultant in A/E bleeped me, the Surgical Registrar, directly bypassing the Surgical House Officer. The patient had to be seen immediately by me, he thought.

When I saw the man he was in so much pain that I had to give him an injection of intravenous morphine before I could have a conversation with him or I could examine him. Usually surgeons would like to withhold pain-killing injections prior to arriving at a diagnosis so that true clinical findings like tenderness on palpation will not be masked. He looked very ill.

When he was able to talk to me he said, "The pain in my tummy and chest came only after I had an episode of vomiting. I never had any serious illness in the past apart from indigestion on and off. I don't know if something I ate didn't agree with me but I vomited several times and the last one was a violent vomiting. This pain started straight after that." He was a smoker and had the usual smoker's cough. This time after his usual brief coughing he started vomiting for some unknown reason.

I could see that he had difficulty in breathing as he was talking to me. On examining his abdomen there was some tenderness and it was quite tight and rigid. Most significant finding was 'crepitus' (described as a feeling of crumbling rice crispies on touching the skin) on palpating the upper part of chest wall, just below and above the collar bone and on side of the neck; it was due to air under the subcutaneous tissue (tissue beneath the skin). The Surgeons call it 'surgical emphysema'.

The history of a violent vomiting and the presence of air beneath the skin indicated a rupture of the oesophagus (gullet) or the bronchus (airway). That night the Consultant Surgeon on call was Mr Knight. He was the youngest of the five Consultant Surgeons in the hospital. He was an excellent Surgeon who had spent some time in St. Marks' Hospital to get expertise in gastro-intestinal surgery in general and colo-rectal surgery in particular. I telephoned Mr Knight. He said he would come in straight away.

There were no diagnostic tools except a plain X-ray and the blood tests. A CT scan would have been most helpful but none was available in any of the nearby hospitals except in the neurological centre fifty miles away.

Mr Knight agreed with me that it was most likely a perforation of the gullet. He asked me to arrange theatre for emergency surgery. News travels fast. The theatre staff were already aware that some major surgical case was on its way from the A/E. The house officer had sent blood samples for cross matching. I explained to the patient that an immediate operation was necessary. He was more than willing when he signed the consent form.

Mr Knight used a thoraco-abdominal incision, opening the abdomen and chest. Usually, he did his operations very fast but this was a long and drawn out one. The gullet was ruptured and the torn segment had to be excised (cut out). To make up for the lost bit, part of the stomach had to be pulled up and fashioned into a tube. Elective operations have less failure rates than major cases done as emergency procedures. During the operation Mr Knight kept saying that this man's prognosis was bleak. I guess he was just cautioning me, the anaesthetist and the surgical house officer that post-operative care had to be fool proof if the patient was to survive.

As it happened the resection and anastomosis went very well and was better than expected. The patient was in the intensive care for a fortnight. He had a topsy-turvy post-operative recovery. The specimen sent to the laboratory did not show any evidence of cancer but there was evidence of a long standing benign ulcer. It must have been the force of vomiting which caused the perforation in the gullet at the site of the previous ulcer even though spontaneous perforation of oesophagus was a very rare occurrence. He was discharged home after three weeks.

THE GENTLEMAN WHO REFUSED
TO BE SEEN

I have had only a very few cases from the outpatient clinics which linger in my memory as remarkable. One of them was a fifty-eight year old man, Mr Whitehead, who refused to see me.

He was referred by his General Practitioner because he requested 'the snip', the vasectomy operation for family planning. He was older than the average man requesting a vasectomy. Obviously personal circumstances of people differ from one man to another. If somebody requests a vasectomy it needs to be considered favourably unless there is a strong reason not to do so. There was a time when the wife or the partner also had to agree for the procedure to go ahead but now it is not essential and people don't always go to the outpatient clinics with their partners.

Mr Whitehead, when his name was called, opened the door of the clinic room. When he saw me, he immediately said to the nurse, "I don't want to see him. He is not Mr Morrison. Is he?"

The nurse was in an awkward position. She was of Caucasian origin just like Mr Whitehead and she wanted to defend me, and argue the case for him to see me.

She said, "Mr Morrison is not here today. Mr Jay is doing the clinic on his behalf. Even if he was here Mr Morrison could not have seen all the patients by himself."

Mr Whitehead almost shouted, pointing his finger at me, "I don't want him to see me," making it very clear that he didn't want to be seen by a man of Indian origin.

I was only pleased that I will have one patient less to see in a busy clinic. I jumped in and said, "It is perfectly all right. Mr Whitehead can come back another day when Mr Morrison is around."

The nurse was pleased that I was not offended. She said, "All right, come to the reception desk with me. We will make another appointment so that you can see Mr Morrison."

It is not uncommon that patients come to a clinic expecting to see the named Consultant in their appointment letter and find that they are going to be seen by someone else. The person seeing them may be more senior and experienced than the Consultant but it is always a mild disappointment for them when they walk into the room and find somebody else other than the man or woman mentioned in their appointment letter. However, often they are aware that an appointment with a specialist for which they waited so long cannot be dismissed in the hope of seeing the Consultant himself at a much later date. In these situations most patients are prepared to be seen so that investigations can go ahead and a diagnosis can be made earlier than later.

There are, however, some people who are prejudiced. They may have had a bad experience when they saw an Indian doctor in the past. They may hold racist views and be adamant that they will be seen only by white doctors.

My view is that if a patient insists that he wants to see only the Consultant in charge, or a man of white colour so that he will be relaxed in the consultation process, his wish should be respected. I wrote in the case note that the patient refused to see me and therefore another appointment has been arranged for him to see Mr Morrison.

I forgot about this episode till after a few weeks when Mr Morrison told me about his encounter with Mr Whitehead.

Mr Morrison would always look at the case notes to see whom he was going to see next when he was seeing patients in a clinic. That day he saw that the next patient was a Mr Whitehead who had refused to see Mr Jay a few weeks ago and this appointment was the second appointment arranged subsequently. He asked the nurse to call the patient.

Mr Whitehead ambled in cheerfully. Mr Morrison asked him, "Why didn't you see Mr Jay when you came last time?"

The man was taken aback because he didn't expect that question. Immediately he said, shooting from the hip, "He was a horrible man with an attitude."

"Why do you say that?" Mr Morrison asked.

Being put on the spot, the man instantly said, "When my name was called and I came in, he was sitting back in his chair and smoking a cigarette. That is not the way to behave. Is it?"

Mr Morrison looked at him and said, "Mr Jay is a non-smoker. He was not smoking when you came in. The nurse who called your name was with you when you came in. She didn't see him smoking."

The man insisted. "I swear that he was smoking when I came in."

The conversation ended there. After examining him and explaining to him the pros and cons of a vasectomy, Mr Morrison told the patient that his name had been added to the waiting list for vasectomy and that all the vasectomies done in that hospital were done by Mr Jay.

MrWhitehead left without a word. He must have had the vasectomy done elsewhere.

THE YOUNG MAN IN A MOTORBIKE ACCIDENT

Adam Kelechuku was a nineteen-year-old who loved his motorbike, which had been a birthday present from his dad, the managing director of a private company. His mother was English and father of Nigerian origin. Whenever he had a chance, he would take the bike out for a ride. He had it only a few weeks and the novelty and excitement had not worn off.

That evening he heard that one of his friends, Jason, fell down from the ladder, broke his ankle and was taken to the A/E Department of the district General Hospital. He decided to pay him a visit and mounted his motor bike. Parking in the hospital car park was tedious for car owners and Adam was delighted that there was no difficulty for him to park his bike there.

Jason's accident was not all that serious. In fact he had only some torn ligaments around the ankle. The X-ray didn't show any fracture. The rumour of a broken ankle was not true. Adam laughed and joked and teased Jason for coming to the hospital for a bruise on the ankle. He suggested that Jason was just a wimp and a softie. The nurses in the A/E looking after Jason noticed this young guy taking the Mickey out of his friend and told him off for being insensitive.

The young nurse attending Jason said to herself, "This Adam guy is rather dishy, isn't he?" He was indeed a very good looking young man. Shortly after, Adam took leave of his friend and the nurses and got on his bike for his ride back home.

The accident happened not far from the hospital. The driver of the car which hit the bike had not probably looked in his wing mirror. Adam was trying to overtake the car when the car moved to its right. There were a lot of people around on the road and an ambulance was on the scene within minutes.

The nurses in the A/E were shocked to see that the young man with whom they had a conversation barely half an hour ago was brought in an ambulance after an accident.

Adam didn't have a head injury. He was fully conscious and talking about what happened in spite of excruciating chest pain. The Senior House Officer in Surgery, Matt, who was called to see him was a very competent and diligent doctor. He noticed that Adam had difficulty in breathing and that it was a case of severe chest injury. He bleeped me, the on call Surgical Registrar, and asked me to get to the A/E as soon as possible.

By the time I arrived, a chest X-ray was done. There was no CT scan in the hospital. The X-ray showed several rib fractures and a haemo-pneumothorax (trapped air and blood in pleura, the lining of the lung). No wonder why the lad had difficulty in breathing. I told him that it was necessary to insert a drainage tube into the chest to relieve the trapped air because his breathing was becoming more and more laboured. He readily agreed.

He asked me, "Will I be all right doctor?"

"Of course," I said, even when I knew fully well the seriousness of the situation. It is imperative that an anxious patient is reassured as much as possible.

When I inserted the chest drain, after infiltrating the area with local anaesthetic, air and blood emerged as was expected. His blood pressure was normal, the pulse was rapid. Matt had already sent blood samples to the laboratory and started an intravenous drip. Soon we commenced him on blood transfusion because he was losing a lot of blood through the chest drain and his pulse rate was getting more rapid even though the blood pressure was still stable. He was in a state of clinical shock even though his young athletic body was handling the situation reasonably well for the time being.

I telephoned the Consultant Surgeon on call, Mr MacArthur. He was a well-known Vascular Surgeon. In fact he was the only recognised, dedicated Vascular Surgeon in the hospital even though there was another Surgeon, a General Surgeon, with an interest in vascular surgery. I told him about Adam and that he was losing blood at an unacceptable and alarming rate. He asked me to arrange theatre for immediate operation and said that he would join us in theatre. In the meantime, Adam's relatives had arrived. His father was at work but his mother and younger brother were there with the grandparents. I briefed them about the seriousness of the injuries and that we had to try and stop the bleeding as soon as possible. Adam was fully conscious, even though his blood pressure was now slowly dropping; he himself signed the consent form for the operation.

We had him anaesthetised and ready on the operation table at lightning speed. The Consultant anaesthetist on call had come in. Mr MacArthur did a generous, long incision for good access and opened up the chest. There was a torrent of bleeding when the large clot covering the torn blood vessels was removed to inspect the area. Mr MacArthur had not anticipated the ferocity of the bleeding and the amount of blood loss. He tried gallantly to stem the tide of blood with the pressure of large swabs but without success. I tried my level best to help him but all our efforts were in vain. The anaesthetist tried to keep the transfusion going. Within a short time twenty-five units of blood were transfused.

The major blood vessels inside the chest had been avulsed and in the welling up of blood that ensued nothing could be done to save the young man.

It was the saddest day of my surgical career. Mr MacArthur was lost for words, like a man who just had a knockout blow and didn't know what had hit him. He was a nationally reputed Vascular Surgeon who was completely helpless in spite of his considerable skills and expertise. To lose a young man in the theatre under those circumstances was devastating to us all, especially me after I had reassured him before the operation when he asked me, "*Will I be all right doctor?*"

I didn't realise that I was silently weeping, till Matt, our SHO, put a hand on my shoulder and tried to console me. He had witnessed my conversation with the young man and my answer to him, "*Of course you will be all right.*" He understood how sad I felt at that time.

Often people don't realise that, doctors, are fellow human beings just like the rest of the population and we also genuinely experience emotional turmoil when faced with tragedies like this. Often we have to mask our feelings not to make matters worse for the relatives and we have to help them cope with their loss.

Mr MacArthur volunteered to speak to the relatives because he knew I was not in a state to take on that responsibility. To this very day, from time to time, I remember the face of that handsome young man involved in that fatal bike accident twenty-five years ago.

THE LADY WHO HAD A PERFORATED COLONIC DIVERTICULUM

The seventy-five year old lady, Mrs Wood, said that she had pain in the left side of her lower abdomen for a few days. She also had constipation followed by diarrhoea. In fact she had investigations for these symptoms previously and a barium enema had shown diverticular disease of the sigmoid colon (the last part of the large bowel before the rectum). What brought her to the Accident and Emergency (A/E) Department was the severe pain in the abdomen which was much worse than previously.

She said, "The pain is so severe that it hurts when I move. It is now all over the tummy. It was only in the left side to begin with." She went on to say, "This is very much like what I had last year when I came here and had to have an operation to remove my gall bladder."

Thankfully her old notes were available. I was astonished to read that the previous year I was the surgeon who performed the operation she was talking about! The operation notes were written by me. Even though I didn't recognise Mrs Wood, the case notes clearly showed that she was brought to the hospital as an emergency case and that she had undergone surgery. The patient did not recognise me either. In emergency situations patients don't always remember who did their previous operations. It may well be that I was away on holiday for a few days during her post-operative stay in hospital otherwise she would have seen me during daily ward rounds for seven days till she was discharged. According to the notes I had written, she had a perforated gall bladder after a bout of nasty cholecystitis (inflammation of the gall bladder). I had written that the removal of the gall bladder was easier than expected because of the acute inflammation had made the tissues oedematous, thereby facilitating the dissection. I recalled that there were two cases of gall bladder perforations the previous year and that this lady was one of them, even though I had not recognised her when I saw her first.

On examining her it was clear that she was genuine in her impression that this was like the problem she had last year. She had all the signs and symptoms of an acute abdomen like last time. I explained to her that she had to undergo an operation to diagnose the problem. I didn't have to tell her that she had only one gall bladder and because it was removed last year the cause of her current symptoms was from something different. She knew that already. When obtaining her consent for the operation I reminded her that if there was perforation of the large bowel due to diverticulitis, she might need to have a colostomy.

On exploration of the abdomen through a mid-line incision it was confirmed that she had perforation of the sigmoid colon. It was where she had the diverticulitis. There was no evidence of malignancy in the bowel or anywhere else. The rest of the abdominal organs also felt normal.

The Consultant surgeon on call that day was Mr Callahan. I knew that he would like me to do a Hartman's procedure in an emergency situation like this. It meant a colostomy had to be fashioned in the left side of lower abdomen. When the acute and dangerous phase was over he would do an elective operation to re-join the bowel and get rid of the colostomy.

I closed off the rectal stump using the stapler gun and fashioned a colostomy in the left lower abdomen. A peritoneal lavage was done using normal saline, and the abdomen closed after leaving a vacuum drain in place. The Anaesthetist had already given the patient the appropriate antibiotic prophylaxis as per my request. Mrs Wood had an excellent recovery and after about a week she was discharged home.

It was beyond belief that I operated on the same lady for perforation of her gall bladder as well as perforation of her sigmoid colon in the period of my two year contract in that hospital.

THE YOUNG LADY WHO CAME FOR A DAY CASE PROCEDURE

Susan was adamant that she didn't want a procedure under local anaesthesia.

"I don't want to know what is happening," she said. "I want to go under and wake up when it is all over."

She had only an unsightly birth mark on her arm. She made clear that she would rather be asleep when it was to be removed. It stood out whenever she went swimming or sun bathing and she was fed up with people asking her why she didn't have it removed. She had only got married recently and was planning to travel the world with her husband.

Nowadays lumps and bumps which are not suspicious of any malignant potential are not removed in many hospitals unless there is another strong indication for their removal. Even if a doctor decides to offer surgical removal, he has to fill in an application form explaining the reason why and there has to be prior approval from a committee who decides on each case according to its merit. This incident happened in 1980s well before 'low priority procedure approval' committees were in vogue.

Susan came with her husband to the hospital in the morning but he went to work as usual because it was only a day case procedure. He would come back in the evening to collect her and take her home. She was a very healthy woman without any history of previous illnesses or current medication. She did not have any known allergies either. On the day of the operation she was seen by the Pre-Registration House Officer who assessed her and got her to sign the consent form.

The Consultant Anaesthetist for all patients on the operation list that morning was Dr Ramsey. He was a Senior Registrar in the North London training programme till three months ago. Since being appointed to this hospital as a Consultant it was his first day of work. He had a short break of three months before he took on the responsibility of a Consultant Anaesthetist.

Susan was on the list as the first patient because she was a day case and had to recover from anaesthesia and be ready to be collected when her husband came in the evening. The rest of the cases were patients who had to have more complicated surgery. They were all inpatients.

I was in the doctors' sitting room talking to the Consultant Surgeon, Mr Reid, in charge of the morning's list. In these conversations, the subjects covered would be emergency admissions, patients recovering in the ward from the previous operations, national politics, the state of the NHS etc. He was a General Surgeon with an interest in vascular surgery and that day he asked, "Are you on call today?"

I answered, "Yes."

"If you are not too busy in the evening could you do an above knee amputation on Mr Chopra. The embolectomy done last night when he presented as an emergency did not work. The problem is that it was too late by the time he presented himself to the hospital. It is a pity."

Mr Chopra was a chain smoker whose blood vessels were already compromised all over when he presented with a large clot in his artery. The on call team tried their best to save his leg by removing the clot but it was a futile attempt and the leg was already beyond redemption by the time he presented himself in the Casualty Department. The unenviable job of the amputation had now fallen into my lap. Obviously the patient's life would be in danger if someone didn't get on with it and remove the leg as soon as possible.

I volunteered and said, "Okay, Mr Reid, I will do it in the evening. There won't be space in any of the routine lists which are full all week."

While we were talking, we realised that the first patient on the list was not on the table yet. Otherwise the nurses or ODA (operating Department assistant) would have come and called us. We decided to go and have a peep into the anaesthetic room to see if there was a problem, even at the risk of incurring the displeasure of the Anaesthetist. Most Anaesthetists hated it when the Surgeons, or anybody else, peeped through the door of the anaesthetic room when patients were being put to sleep.

As we were gingerly opening the door to the anaesthetic room, it was shocking to see the ODA was doing cardiac message on Susan and the Anaesthetist was holding the oxygen mask in place. The nurses in theatre were also unaware of what was happening. In fact it was quite timely that we decided to check on proceedings in the anaesthetic room. The Anaesthetist was relieved to see us coming in. He said that the patient reacted to the injection he gave and she slowly went into cardiac arrest. After a while, I took over the cardiac massage. Even after another ten minutes, when we stopped the chest compressions the femoral pulse could not be felt. We continued the chest compressions to keep the circulation going.

Whenever I was in a tight corner and my patients were in danger I had the habit of praying for them silently in my thoughts. I prayed fervently asking God that our efforts to save this young lady be successful. Mr Reid took over the cardiac compressions from me and after ten minutes the ODA took over from him. In the meantime the Anaesthetist had intubated Susan. He had given several intravenous injections to reverse any allergy and to get her cardiac contractions going again. After another few minutes of further chest compressions her heart started contracting on its own as evidenced by the ECG leads and the femoral pulse.

There was a collective sigh of relief in the room. Gradually she was deemed well enough to be transferred to the ICU We had to cancel the last patient on the list. The patient who got cancelled was told the reason and he was gracious enough to be understanding. He didn't make a fuss and he was given another date for his surgery before he left.

When Susan's husband came to collect her from hospital in the evening he had the shock of his life to find her in the ICU. When the situation was explained to him he was more than relieved that she was alive though still seriously ill. The prolonged chest compressions had resulted in a couple of broken ribs but it was managed conservatively. Being a young lady Susan came through her ordeal remarkably well and was moved to the general surgical ward the next day and allowed home after another couple of days.

THE CASE OF THE REFUGEE

After the two wars in the Middle East, there have been a number of refugees who got legal permission to stay in the UK. Occasionally I used to see some of them in the clinic.

One day one Mr Yousef Makar, who described himself as a refugee was seen in the outpatient clinic. He complained of a lump in the testicle which he had for a few years. He said he was concerned because it was becoming bigger. On examination he had a benign cyst on the left epididymis (the tubular structure above the testis) but the testes on both sides were entirely normal.

I explained to the man, "This is only a harmless cyst, a collection of fluid in a thin sac. You had it for a long time. There is no need for you to undergo an operation. Occasionally after scrotal surgery patients do develop complications like infection or a large blood clot in the scrotal sac. Even if this cyst is removed, another similar one can develop in the same area after a while."

He was not pleased. He insisted that he wanted it removed because it was becoming bigger.

I felt obliged to place him on the waiting list for excision of the left epididymal cyst. I told Mr Makar that the procedure would be done as a day case under general anaesthesia and that there would not be any routine follow up if all went well. I also said that there was the average waiting time for a procedure was about twelve weeks.

He left the outpatient clinic very happy.

About three months later Sam, the receptionist at our outpatient clinic, told me that there was a post-operative patient who rang them up continually asking for an appointment with me. He also said that the patient was now living twenty-five miles away and was enquiring about the taxi fare because he was on income support and he couldn't afford to pay for a taxi. I declined to get drawn into the issue of his taxi fare but told the receptionist that I was happy to review him in the clinic.

On the day of his appointment Mr Makar arrived promptly. He walked in to my clinic room, limping and heavily leaning on a walking stick.

I asked him, "Why are you limping? You were all right when you came to see me last time."

He replied, "Oh. I developed a severe back problem since. I can hardly walk."

I examined him and found that the wound on his scrotum had healed completely. I was baffled as to why he came back to see me. We don't give follow up appointment for day case procedures like the one he had unless there were some complication.

Mr Makar said that he was very pleased and that he didn't have any problem after surgery. He came just to say that he was grateful. He then produced small box of chocolate which he put on my table. I told him that I didn't want anything from him as a reward. I had not even done the operation. All I did was place him on the waiting list. It was one of my colleagues who carried out the operation and the patient knew that. He just wouldn't listen and he completely ignored what I said.

Instead he produced a printed claim form and asked me, "Could you please sign this form because I came from twenty-five miles away in a taxi. I will get the taxi fare back because I am on benefits."

I was not impressed with this man bringing me a box of chocolate and trying to get me to sign a claim form for him. I said I was sorry that I couldn't sign any form for him for a journey he made which was totally unnecessary. Surprisingly he didn't become angry or abusive. He was very polite and pleasant still and he said, "That is all right doctor. I understand." He left after thanking me again.

After a few days our receptionist, Sam, asked me, "Do you remember Mr Yousef Makar, the man who came to see you the other day whose claim form you didn't sign?"

I said that I remembered him very well.

Sam continued. "When he failed to get you to sign the form he approached me and asked me to sign it. I refused to sign it because you hadn't signed it. He left the clinic, put a false signature on your behalf and took it to the cashier's office and got the taxi fare. When the Cashier went for his lunch he saw this man walking cheerfully without any walking stick or any limp. He then got very suspicious and telephoned me to find if we had signed the form or he signed it himself. When he confirmed that the guy had used false signatures, the Cashier informed the police and Mr Makar was under investigation by the police."

Sam warned me that the Police may contact me for a statement.

THE CASE OF THE BLADDER FLUKE

About twenty years ago one day I was doing a ward round to see the patients for operation that afternoon and obtain consent from them when I came across a young man who was listed for a Trans Urethral Resection of Bladder Tumour (TURBT). Mike Baker was only twenty-six years old. He was a bit too young to have a bladder tumour, I thought.

Then I remembered the case of the twenty-eight year old German student, who was a heavy smoker, who had presented himself to the Accident and Emergency Department with heavily blood-stained urine. Later on when he was investigated in the Urology Department, he was found to have a nasty high grade tumour of the bladder. Most common cause for frank blood in urine is a urinary infection but bladder tumours have to be ruled out especially in the absence of infection and especially in the older age group.

I asked him, "Are you a smoker?" (In 50 - 60% of men with bladder cancer in the UK, the cause is smoking).

Mike replied, "I have never smoked in my life."

When I looked through the case notes I could see that the initial telescopic inspection of Mike's urinary bladder, under local anaesthesia, was done by one of the experienced Registrars. He had drawn a diagram to show what he had seen and where in the bladder he had seen it. I explained to the patient how the operation was done through a telescope placed in the Urethra, the natural tube through which urine comes out. I told him that there won't be any wound outside the bladder but he had to put up with a catheter placed in the bladder to drain blood stained urine till the urine became clear when it would be removed.

I also explained the possible complications of the procedure. He agreed and signed the consent form. He asked me about the prognosis if it was cancer. I replied that only the pathology report could give us confirmation if it was a tumour and what the prognosis would be.

The hospital was a small cottage hospital about seven miles away from the main hospital where we worked. The patients were supposed to be reasonably fit and well if they were to be posted for operation in the cottage hospital. These cases were done mainly to relieve the pressure on the theatre in the main hospital where all acute emergencies and trauma cases had to be done. Those of us who worked in the small hospital loved the place. The Ward Staff and the Theatre Staff were excellent. They were very caring and friendly and they took pride in looking after the patients sent there.

Mike Baker had General Anaesthesia. When I first inspected the bladder with the telescope, I could see what was described as a bladder tumour exactly where the Registrar had drawn it in his diagram. It looked like a very small strawberry.

It didn't look like the typical appearance of a bladder tumour. In any case I removed it with the resectoscope, the instrument designed to do the procedure, and sent the specimen for analysis in the laboratory. I thought that what I saw looked very much like a parasitic infection called Schistosomiasis, commonly known as 'bladder fluke'. The condition is commonly seen in West Africa and the Middle East in addition to a number of other countries. Swimming or bathing in fresh water streams or rivers is how human infestation of the parasites takes place. I suspected it because I had seen a similar appearance during a bladder inspection in a patient who had Schistosomiasis a few years ago in another Hospital.

When I saw Mike in the ward after the operation list was over, he was already sitting up and chatting with the nurses. I asked him if he had travelled overseas in the recent past. He said that he had a backpacking holiday trip to West Africa and had taken bath in some rivers and streams. I told him about my finding in his bladder and my suspicion that it could simply be a parasitic infection. Of course he had to wait for the laboratory report to find out exactly what it was that I removed.

A couple of weeks later when I saw the Senior Consultant Urologist in the Urology Office he told me that in the morning clinic he had seen Mike Baker and that the diagnosis was Schistsomiasis according to the pathology report from the laboratory. Obviously the young man was delighted because all he needed was a course of tablets to get rid of the 'bladder fluke' parasitic infection!

THE MAN WITH SWELLING ABOVE
HIS TESTICLE

The increased awareness of the risk of testicular cancer in young men has led to more and more men approaching their GPs to be checked out. There have also been more referrals to Urologists from GPs on the 'two-week' cancer referral pathway. These are very welcome developments which have taken place in recent times.

A few years ago I saw a thirty-eight year old man, Clint Walker, in the clinic who complained of a swelling above his right testis. He was a married man with two children and his wife was present during the consultation. He said that he was self-employed. Apparently he had started his own business a few years ago and was now the owner of a thriving company. He didn't have any previous illness. He was not on any medication. He was concerned about the swelling that he went to his GP promptly and got an Ultrasound scan organised privately, instead of waiting for the hospital appointment. The scan was reported to be normal. Still he was concerned that something was not right.

Mr Walker was six foot four inches tall and a healthy looking man. On examination both his testes felt normal. There was no tenderness on palpating the testes. Just above the right testes there was an irregular feeling lump on the epididymis, the tubular structure above and attached to the testis. There was no tenderness on it. It was not a smooth cyst, which would be the case most often.

I asked him, "Have you had any severe pain in the area before you noticed a lump there?"

He said he didn't. Inflammation of the epididymis is common after bacterial or even viral infections. Occasionally a simple Urinary Infection may be the cause and sometimes Chlamydia or other sexually transmitted infections also can cause the same clinical picture. Mr Walker was emphatic that he had no such problems in the past. Often the swelling is as a result of the vasectomy the patient had in the past but he had not undergone a vasectomy. His wife had undergone sterilisation of the Fallopian tubes after their last child was born.

I explained to the husband and wife that the testes were normal on ultrasound scan and clinical examination. The swelling on the epididymis was seen on ultrasound and the radiologist described it as a thickening probably from previous infection. I told the husband and wife that malignant lumps of the epididymis were very rare indeed and that most of the swellings there were benign. However, I said I would see them again in two weeks to see if the swelling was becoming any bigger.

His wife stood up and said, "Thank you doctor."

Mr Clint Walker was still seated. He asked me, "Why do you think I feel so tired of late? I also have periodic discomfort in my right testis and occasional backache." He went on to say, "It is said that coming events cast their shadows. I think some mischief is afoot."

I felt a bit uneasy that he was still seated there and alerting me about his tiredness and raising his concerns about some impending danger. Experience has taught me to be 'switched on' in these delicate consultations. This man, a self-employed successful owner of his own company is sitting there and telling me that he feels tired of late. He also complaints of pain in testis as well as some back ache. I wondered. What is happening here? This man doesn't fit the picture of a hypochondriac.

Something was not right, as he said. I decided that he deserved further investigation in the form of a CT scan. I told him, "Mr Walker, if you have back ache and pain in the right testis from time to time, it may well be that you have kidney stones. The pain from kidney stones sometimes is felt in the testis and it is known as a referred pain. Let me arrange a CT scan which will give us some information about the kidneys."

What I didn't tell them was the CT scan could also show any tumour in the kidneys. Kidney tumours are sometimes called 'silent killers' because they may not give any tangible symptoms and are notorious for late presentation to doctors. I wanted to rule out that as well any lymph nodes or any other abnormalities in the abdomen.

Here was a man with genuine concern that something has gone wrong because he felt ill, has had back ache and occasional pain in testis in addition to an irregular lump on the epididymis.

I arranged an urgent CT scan and gave him an appointment to see me in two weeks so that he doesn't get lost in the system. I asked the nurse helping me in the outpatient clinic to fax the request for the CT scan to the X-ray Department indicating that he had a follow up appointment in two weeks and the investigation had to be done before that date.

Two weeks later, Mr Clint Walker came back to see me. His wife also was with him. The result of the CT scan was pinned to front of the case notes by the nurse in charge of the clinic. The scan report showed no evidence of any stones in the kidneys or ureter. There was no other abnormality reported in the kidneys but there was mention of some enlarged lymph nodes in the abdomen.

I decided to examine Mr Walker again. The swelling on his epididymis was only slightly larger than before. It was not a cyst. It was irregular in outline and I felt that it could be a tumour, even though malignant tumours of the epididymis were extremely rare.

With the computerisation of the hospitals, each room in the outpatient clinic had a computer so that doctors could access X-rays, Scans, and blood results easily and review them on the computer in front of them. When people complain about the huge amount of money being spent on the NHS they don't give allowance for the huge strides in modernisation that have taken place in the last ten years and the enormous cost involved to keep healthcare in this country comparable to or better than other countries and yet free at the point of delivery here in the UK.

I finished examining Mr Walker and took my seat in front of the computer on my desk. I logged myself in and looked at the CT scan on the screen. The idea was to double check that the name on the report was Mr Walker's and that it was not a report filed wrongly in his name. The hospital number and other details were all correct. Even though I was not trained to look at or report on CT scans, I was curious to have a look at the scan myself.

There was no evidence of any abnormality in the kidneys. However I noticed that there were several enlarged lymph nodes in the abdomen by the sides of the big blood vessels as was casually mentioned in the report. That would explain the man's back ache and his feeling generally unwell. I knew that this was a very significant finding.

Thankfully we had regular Multi-Disciplinary Meetings (MDM) every week in the hospital where the Surgeons, Radiologists (experts on X-rays and scans) and Oncologists (cancer specialist physicians) would present complicated cases and collectively decide the appropriate management for the individual patient. I decided to discuss Mr Walker's CT scan and his examination findings in the meeting. He was given an appointment to come back and see me in one week by which time I would have discussed his case in the MDM.

The review of the CT scan was immensely helpful. The Radiologists and Oncologists present unanimously confirmed that this was a case of Lymphoma, a malignant condition of the lymph nodes and that the swelling on the epididymis was only a manifestation of the generalised disease.

The recommendation of the MDM was to refer Mr Walker urgently to the Oncology/Haematology specialist Physicians. In two days' time when I saw him and his wife in the clinic I explained to them that the CT scan was reviewed and the recommendation of the meeting was to refer Mr Walker to the physicians. Obviously they were very upset about diagnosis but they were also pleased that a diagnosis was reached and not missed!

The patients' theory that coming events cast their shadows was proved right!

THE BRAVE LITTLE GIRL

Several years ago I worked as a Registrar in Accident and Emergency Department in a very busy hospital in England, for one year. There was only one other Registrar in A/E and we had to work twenty-four hours continuously every other day and seventy-two hours continuously every other week end. This work pattern was called a one in two rota and it is now illegal.

One day a five-year-old little girl, Sophie, was brought to the casualty minor injuries unit. The little finger of her left her hand was crushed when her father closed the door of the car without realising that her hand was in the way.

When I saw her she was holding her Teddy bear close to her chest. She was not crying. That surprised me. The left hand was bandaged with a clean kerchief. Her parents told me that the last digit of her little finger was crushed and was hanging by the skin. When I asked if I could have a look at her finger she agreed.

After cleaning away the matted blood and clots I could see that the last digit of the finger was severed off and was hanging by a small piece of torn skin.

Her mother said, "She cried when the accident happened but on the way here she was quiet. May be because last time she was brought here, she was pleased that she was well treated."

From her case record I could see that she was brought to the A/E a few months ago when she had a 'pulled elbow'. The condition is a dislocation of the head of radius, one of the two long bones of the forearm. It happens when parents play with their children, lifting them up holding them by their wrists and sometimes swinging them around. The child cries and refuses to move the forearm when parents suspect something is wrong and takes him or her to the A/E. The reduction of the dislocation is simple. The doctor holds the child's forearm and gently turns it into a supine position, the palm of the hand facing upwards. This gentle manoeuvre solves the problem and the head of the radius is back in its normal position. The child is very happy because the problem is solved instantly without much discomfort. This was what happened last time Sophie was brought and her mother thought that it was that experience which gave her the confidence to remain calm. I did not remember the child and from case notes I could see that it was Mr Desai, my colleague Registrar, who dealt with the case at that time

There was only one Consultant, Mr Shah, in the A/E and he was always in charge. He used to tell me, "Mr Jay, I am married to my bleep." He was in the Department when Sophie was brought.

He told me, "This little girl will be here in the hospital for very long time today because the Orthopaedic doctors are so busy with major injuries and operations. She may not get seen all day and night if we refer her to them. This is a crush injury of the last digit of her little finger. She has confidence in you because she thinks you reduced her 'pulled elbow' last time. To her Mr Desai and Mr Jay would look alike. Why don't you give her a local injection and tidy up her finger for her. Remove the severed digit and cover the stump with a flap sutured over it. Do it in our minor theatre here in A/E so that she can go home and have her dinner."

Mr Shah had his Senior Registrar training in a famous teaching hospital in the North of England. He used to speak highly of that hospital and the A/E Department there. Apparently they used to do burr holes on the skulls of head injury patients, in the A/E theatre, to evacuate clots from brain! He wanted to get as many things done in the A/E if possible. His policy was to reduce all Colles fractures of the wrists (which result in the typical 'dinner fork' deformity) in A/E under local anaesthesia, so that Orthopaedic surgeons could deal with broken hips and other major injuries in the main theatres in the hospital. It was winter time and people were falling over and injuring themselves because of heavy snow fall the previous couple of days. That was why I myself had to reduce eight Colles fractures in a row, one after another, when I was on call the previous day. The Senior House Officer would assist but the Registrar had to do the reduction of the fracture and immobilisation of the wrist.

Mr Shah asked the parents if it was all right to sort out the problem under local anaesthesia. They knew that it was impossible to re-attach the severed last digit of their daughter's little finger. They agreed and signed the consent form.

Sophie was moved to the theatre in the A/E where major suturing and other procedures were done.

I asked her, "Sophie, will you let me do an injection in your little finger to make it better? You are a brave girl aren't you?"

The sweet little girl looked at me and said, "Yes."

She was allowed to keep her Teddy bear close to her chest, holding it with her right hand, when she was lying on the operation table. The left arm was moved away from the body and secured on a 'hand rest' attached to the table. There was a nurse sitting by her side and talking to her. I used a tiny needle to do the infiltration of local anaesthetic.(It takes longer to complete the infiltration if a very small needle is used but it is kinder to the child). She flinched and cried for a minute or two when the needle hit the skin and the anaesthetic was infiltrated. Soon, she was back to normal.

Sophie, this amazing child, lay there quietly throughout the procedure when I cleaned the wound with an iodine based solution, tidied the stump of her finger using the bone cutter and scissors, and fashioned a flap over the bone with absorbable sutures. Most of the time, she was engaged in a private conversation with her Teddy bear!

When I finished the procedure and her finger was bandaged I told the parents that we would like her to have antibiotic prophylaxis for five days and they agreed. The child had immunisation against tetanus already. A follow up appointment was given to bring the child back for inspection of the finger and the family was allowed home.

When they were about to leave her mother asked Sophie, "What do you say to the doctor?"

The little girl, the pain in her finger still numbed by the local anaesthetic, said with a smile, "Thank you doctor."

I told her, "Sophie, you are the bravest little girl I have ever seen."

I meant every word of what I said.

THE YOUNG LADY WITH
THE URETERIC STONE

I had a special interest in Urology even when I did my one year Pre-Registration House Officer job after my graduation. We could choose which surgical speciality we wanted to be attached for two weeks. I decided to have some basic knowledge of Urology and got myself enrolled in the Urology unit.

Later on in life, after the FRCS, I decided that I wanted to pursue a career in Urology. I guess it was the opportunity to do endoscopic surgery as well as open operations which was attractive to me. Most laparoscopic operations done in other specialities at present were not in existence at that time.

About fifteen years ago, Liza, a twenty-four year old lady, was seen in the Accident and Emergency Department with severe colicky abdominal pain.

She said, "I have never had any pain like this before in my life. It is worse than labour pains."

She had two children by the time she was twenty-four. She was a streetwise young lady and she had no hesitation to say that she was a smoker and that occasionally she smoked cannabis.

Her symptoms were highly suggestive of a ureteric colic (the colicky pain experienced when a stone moves from the kidney into the ureter, the natural tube connecting kidney to urinary bladder). She was not allergic to contrast medium and therefore an intravenous urogram (IVU) was done to establish the diagnosis. When the films were looked at, she was found to have an eight-millimetre stone in the ureter. It was seen to cause partial obstruction to the kidney.

The patient was admitted to the Urology ward after she was given an injection for pain relief. That evening the emergency operation list was full and it was decided to add her on to the elective Urology operation list the next day for a ureteroscopy (inspection of the ureter with a telescope) and extraction of the stone.

I happened to be in the theatre the next day when this lady was brought for the procedure. The radiographers were available in theatre if we wanted some imaging during the procedure to localise the stone. Usually we didn't require them because the stone could be directly seen with the telescope inserted into the ureter.

The Registrar in the theatre with me that day said that he had not done any of these procedures. He had only started his job. I told him to just watch it this time. He would get ample of opportunities to do these cases later on.

It was my habit to check with the Anaesthetist if it was ok to start any operation. I knew that some Anaesthetist would be cross if the Surgeon didn't ask them their permission before starting the case. They may feel that they are ignored. You don't want an Anaesthetist with a bruised ego in theatre to look after your patient. It is also true that the patient may not be ready for the Surgeon to wield the knife if the 'gas man' (or woman) has not given the green light.

When I had the 'go ahead' from the Anaesthetist I asked the nurse assisting me for a cystoscope.

The Registrar asked me immediately, "Can you not just introduce the ureteroscope (the telescope designed to inspect the ureter) straight into the ureter without the cystoscope? It must be easy because this is a woman not a man."

The cystoscope is designed to inspect the bladder.

I replied, "I would inspect the bladder first before introducing the uretersocpe to inspect the ureter. It is always good practice to make sure that the bladder is not harbouring a stone or tumour in it."

"Oh! Come on Mr Jay, she is too young to have a bladder tumour," he said.

He was right to some extent. It was quite unlikely that a woman of twenty-four would have a bladder tumour. However I was not prepared to compromise the safe practice of making sure that the bladder was normal before inspecting the ureter. I used the cystoscope first and inspected the bladder.

The Registar and all those present in the theatre could see, on the theatre television screen, the small bladder tumour I had just seen because there was a camera attached to the telescope. There were gasps of astonishment from all in theatre; nobody had expected to see a bladder tumour in a twenty-four year old who presented with a stone in her ureter. I remembered that she was a heavy smoker. It is well recognised that 45 - 50% of all bladder tumours in women and 50 - 60% in men in the UK were due to smoking. I don't think that the general public is aware of this. The young lads who stand tall among their peers in street corners may consider smoking a cigarette 'cool' and 'trendy'. What they don't realise is that peeing blood is not 'cool' or pleasant.

I managed to introduce the ureteroscope into the ureter and see the stone, break it up remove it completely.

Thereafter I asked the scrub nurse for a resectoscope (the equipment to resect the bladder tumour and remove it without an open operation.). After a slight delay the instrument was brought and I resected and removed the tumor. It was small and it looked superficial, which was the sign of good prognosis. She was discharged home the next day with an appointment for a further inspection of the bladder in three months. When the pathology report was available it was confirmed to be a low grade tumour and that it was superficial with excellent prognosis. Liza was scheduled to have regular follow up.

She did not stop smoking for another few years. For five years she had yearly follow-up without any evidence of recurrence of her tumour or her kidney stone. There was a small tumour seen again in the sixth year. Even though it was a superficial tumour she had bladder installation of some medication to try and prevent future recurrences. Her bladder inspection and surveillance would continue indefinitely. Aggressive bladder tumours of higher grade which invade the bladder muscle do have a worse prognosis.

The guy who taught me to drive a car used to tell me, "Always expect the unexpected when you approach a corner on the road (when there is uncertainty about what lies ahead)." I think it is good advice for doctors dealing with patients and their safety.

THE SIX-WEEK-OLD BABY WITH PROJECTILE VOMITING

The Paediatric hospital was three miles away from the main hospital where I was based, working as a Surgical Registrar. I was frequently asked by paediatricians to go there and see sick children with suspected surgical conditions. I was also asked to go and do 'cut downs' on babies and little children whose intravenous drips got dislodged several times because they were thrashing about crying. I hated going there to the wards with scant facilities to do what was, in reality, a minor surgical procedure: using the knife to make a small incision into the chubby little legs, identify a vein, insert a cannula into it and secure that access as best as you can with sutures, tapes and dressings. Nevertheless, I always obliged because I was aware that babies and little children require intravenous access for fluid replacement and for antibiotics for their survival. All operations, elective or emergency, on children were done in the theatre there. Out of hours, Surgeons as well as nursing and other theatre staff had to come over from the main hospital to open up the theatre there.

One evening I got a call from the locum paediatric Senior House Officer. "Could you please come and see a six-week-old baby with projectile vomiting, who has been diagnosed with pyloric stenosis."

Pyloric stenosis is a condition with which some babies are born. There is muscular thickening of the pylorus, the narrow part of the stomach, which causes obstruction to the smooth passage of food from the stomach to the first part of the intestine. This results in the tell-tale signs of the condition like frequent projectile vomiting and failure of the baby to thrive. A simple operation can cure the condition. In these cases we, the surgeons, act as technical hands. We just go and perform the operation and leave the after care of the baby in the hands of the paediatricians.

I was reminded of the days, several years previously, when I worked in Lancashire with Mr Kirkwood. He was the senior most Surgeon there. The paediatricians loved him because he did all operations on babies with pyloric stenosis under local anaesthesia. He was a firm believer in the usefulness of local anaesthesia, especially in babies in whom general anaesthesia and the subsequent recovery could be hazardous. Thirty-three years ago not all Anaesthetists were trained or experienced to anesthetise babies. He would place the baby in a crucifix position on the operation table in the theatre, secure the arms and legs gently with bandages, so that the baby is not constantly moving during the operation. Then he would get a nurse to sit at the head end of the table and give the baby a lump of sugar wrapped in a gauze piece to suck when he infiltrated the abdominal wall with very low strength local anaesthesia, usually lignocaine. The baby would cry only during this part of the procedure usually. The operation would be performed very quickly thereafter and the baby will be sent to the ward, where the mum can feed the baby shortly afterwards.

Anaesthesia for babies is much improved and far better these days and I suppose some currently practising paediatricians would consider what I described as barbaric.

Of course, this was not Lancashire. That evening there was no paediatric Registrar on call. The locum SHO was an experienced young lady who was covered by the Consultant paediatrician who lived twenty-five miles away because he was based mainly in the District General Hospital there but his contract was also to cover this paediatric unit every other night and every other week end. This was not an ideal arrangement but that was how it was.

I went and saw the baby. The diagnosis being already made and the baby already prepared, I telephoned the theatre staff to come over from the main hospital and open up the theatre facilities for us to do the case. Even though I was confident to do the operation myself, I asked the Consultant Surgeon, Mr Al-Mulaly, who was doing a locum for one of the five Surgeons who was on leave, to come over. The Consultant Anaesthetist also came because it was a baby of six weeks who had to be anaesthetised. He was well experienced in administering general anaesthesia to babies.

The operation itself was a simple on to do. The pylorus of the stomach was identified and the thickened muscle was divided gently with blade of the surgical knife, making sure that the lining of the stomach was not breeched. This was to relieve the obstruction and cure the child. Everything went well and we left the baby in the paediatric ward when it was fully recovered from the anaesthesia.

I returned to the main hospital where there were other cases piling up for my attention. After about two hours later the locum paediatric SHO called me and asked me to go and see the baby we had operated on.

She said, "The wound of the baby is still bleeding and several swabs were changed already because they were getting soaked with blood."

A six-week-old, tiny baby doesn't have a lot of blood to lose and even a small volume loss could push the baby into shock.

I telephoned Mr Al-Mulaly and he said he would join me at the paediatric hospital as soon as he could. I made my way to the paediatric ward as rapidly as possible. On inspecting the wound I could see that the lady SHO was right in her concern. When Mr Al-Mulaly arrived he agreed that the blood loss was not acceptable and we decided to take the baby back to theatre and check if there was any small blood vessel still bleeding, even though we had made sure that there was no bleeding when we had closed the wound.

The Consultant anaesthetist arrived as well as the theatre staff from the main hospital and the baby was on the operation table without delay. We undid the sutures on the abdominal wall and inspected the Wound. There was no bleeding vessel! We inspected the pylorus itself and the muscle we divided. There was no bleeding there either. It was just a generalised oozing from the edges of the abdominal wound. We closed the abdomen again taking extra care to cauterise any area of bleeding. When the baby was safely back in the ward we asked the SHO as well as the Consultant paediatrician to check the baby's clotting factors and rule out any bleeding disorders because we could not identify any cause for the bleeding.

After about two hours, just past midnight, I telephoned the Paediatric SHO to find out how the baby was doing. She said, "The baby continues to bleed, the swabs on the wound dressing getting soaked again. The result of the blood test for clotting factors has not been ready yet."

They were wondering if the baby would need blood transfusion before long.

This was worrying news. I couldn't go to sleep. However, I was pretty certain that there was no need for us to take the child to theatre again and that if we did, we wouldn't find any bleeding vessel.

After another hour I rang the Paediatric Unit again. The SHO told me that the blood tests showed a clotting disorder and the baby was placed in an ambulance and sent to paediatric unit in Guy's hospital about ten minutes ago. It was decided that the baby should be looked after in a Specialist Centre.

THE FIGHT FOR THEATRE TIME

Consultant Surgeons have allotted theatre time to do their elective operations for patients waiting on their waiting lists. They are always conscious of the need to utilise the time fully to reduce the waiting lists. Therefore they guard the time allotted to them with 'hawk eyes' and resent any encroachment on their time by another consultant or anybody else. The ferocity with which they guard their theatre time and space reminds me of the wild life programmes I have watched on television in which the big cats and other animals mark their territory with their scent and fight off the intruders into their domain.

I remember the notorious case in North West England (reported in the National Newspapers and television media) about thirty years ago. Some of the readers of this book may remember it too. A Registrar in Orthopaedics, doing an emergency operation, was still operating when the Consultant Orthopaedic Surgeon came in the morning to do his routine operation list. The furious Consultant, according to the News Paper reports, had an angry confrontation with the Registrar and he allegedly hit the Registrar, who was still wearing his sterile gloves and operating on the patient admitted as emergency case. The story fizzled out in the National Media after the initial novelty and excitement about it had worn off. The Registrar, whom I had met during a course for the FRCS examination previously, could not expect to climb the career ladder any further and ,understandably, he left the UK for United States with his wife who was a trainee Anaesthetist. Even though he had gone to the Accident and Emergency Department and recorded his injuries, as was reported in the News Papers, colleagues and other

Consultants must have persuaded him to drop the case before he left the country.

I witnessed a similar episode where two Consultant Surgeons had a furious argument about the same issue of theatre time which thankfully didn't result in blows. Both of them were tall big guys and a physical encounter would not have been pretty!

I was working with Mr Keith Murray, a Urologist, the junior one of the two Consultant Surgeons involved. The senior man, Mr Stanley Brown, was about to retire in a few months. Both of them were from Scotland and had developed an additional bond of friendship between them. The only problem was that Mr Murray had the morning slot (9 a.m. – 1 p.m.) in theatre on the same day as Mr Brown who had the afternoon operation list (2 p.m. – 6 p.m.). Once in a while, if the morning list was overrunning (not finished by 1 p.m.) Mr Brown would be in a strop because his list will get delayed and he may have to cancel the last case. It is not a pleasant experience to go and tell a patient, who was starving from midnight anticipating surgery that day , that he was cancelled due to lack of theatre time because the guy doing operations in the morning took more time than what he was allotted. Mr Murray would be late in finishing his list probably because one of the cases took more time than expected or because his list that day was overbooked. He would have strived to finish the list so that he didn't have to cancel a patient from his list. This was not a daily occurrence but it happened occasionally.

On that particular day Mr Murray was doing a difficult nephrectomy (removal of one kidney) for cancer as the last case on his morning list. He had deliberately placed the nephrectomy as the last one on the list and done two smaller cases in the beginning of the list because he knew that even if he was over running the theatre time, the major case like removal of a kidney with cancer would not be cancelled. Smaller cases, if left at the end of the list, would be cancelled and not called from the ward. When Mr Brown came in the afternoon to start his routine list, he was told that there would be a significant delay because Mr Murray was still operating on the nephrectomy case. Even after Murray finished his list there would be a delay because the nurses would want to have a break for lunch before starting the afternoon list. Mr Brown was not a happy bunny.

I was assisting Mr Murray in the nephrectomy case when the Anaesthetist Dr Balcombe who was scheduled to anaesthetise patients on the afternoon list wandered in and informed us, rather loudly, that Mr Brown was pacing up and down very upset and angry that he could not start his list on time. Mr Murray ignored those comments and struggled on with the difficult kidney removal.

After ten minutes Mr Brown himself came into the theatre and asked in a rather sarcastic tone, "What is happening, Keith? Do you want me to give you a hand?"

"No, thank you. We are managing all right. Won't be long," said Mr Murray, who was irritated by his colleague's appearance in the theatre and his insincere offer of help. He was a Urological Surgeon and eminently qualified to remove the kidney and he knew that Mr Brown, a General Surgeon with a special interest in Vascular Surgery was simply making a point that the list was unacceptably delayed.

Mr Brown, evidently grumpy, muttered something and walked away. We finished the operation after another twenty minutes. After a quick lunch break and after cleaning up the theatre the nurses agreed that the first patient for the afternoon could be sent for.

Mr Murray finished writing the operation notes, had a cup of coffee and spent some time in the recovery area to see if the patient who had a long operation was alright. Still reeling from the embarrassment of the earlier conversation with Mr Brown, he decided to be a bit naughty and walked into the theatre where Mr Brown was operating.

He asked loudly, "Are you all right Stanley? Would you like me to scrub up and give you a hand?"

There was complete silence in the theatre for a minute or two. Then Mr Brown exploded, "You are totally out of order, you idiot. (I shall not record here the exact words which shot out of the man's lips. It will be inappropriate.) I will certainly report you. You deliberately put the nephrectomy as the last case, encroached on my theatre time and kept me waiting. Now you have the nerve to come in here and irritate me further. I will report you. You wait and see."

"You do just that," Mr Murray replied. "Don't you ever come to the theatre when I am operating and make a scene ever again!"

As I mentioned earlier, there was no physical assault, only verbal abuse, but that confrontation in theatre still lingers in my memory. After a few days all was forgiven and forgotten and they continued to be friends.

The battles for the theatre time are still being played out in theatres up and down the country. The big beasts guard their theatre time with all the guile, the intimidation and the ferocity at their disposal.

THE TEENAGER WHO FELL OFF HER HORSE

I was working as a Senior House Officer (SHO) in orthopaedics at a hospital in England in 1984. One week end I was on call with a locum Registrar covering me. There was no Pre-Registration House Officer in Orthopaedics. The SHO was first on call for all emergency admissions and had to do all the ward-work.

It was a Friday evening. The SHO in Accident and Emergency Department (A/E) bleeped me and asked me for an opinion regarding a nineteen-year-old young lady who had fallen off her horse the previous day. She was seen in the A/E Department at the time because she complained of pain in her neck and was allowed home when the X-rays were all normal and there was no visible injury anywhere. She returned to the A/E because she had persistent pain in her neck.

The SHO who asked me for an opinion was Simon, whose referrals to me previously had been genuine. He was a fairly experienced doctor and I had respect for his clinical judgement. He said, "I am concerned that this teenager has come back with persistent pain and that the previous day when X-rays were done there was no 'odontoid views' done to check the odontoid process of the second vertebra." These views were X-rays done with the patient's mouth in 'open' position.

Simon requested me to see the patient and either discharge her or arrange more X-rays. I said I would go and see her.

The patient was a very sensible young lady who had completed her A levels and just joined the University to read Politics, Philosophy and Economics.

When I examined her the only abnormality I could detect was a slight restriction in the movement of her neck because of pain. I decided that it was best to leave no stone unturned and get additional 'odontoid views' to rule out a fracture of the second vertebra. I sent an X-ray request to the radiology Department.

After about two hours Simon telephoned me to say that my patient was still in the waiting room and that the X-rays were not done. I rang the radiology Department and asked the Radiographer what was happening.

"I had requested some x-rays for a young lady which have not been done yet. The patient has been waiting for a while. Could you please do them as soon as possible?"

The answer of the Radiographer surprised me. She said, "When I saw the request form, I telephoned the Orthopaedic Registrar on call and asked if it was really necessary and he said it was not essential." She continued. "He is here with us in the Department if you want to come and speak to him. We are having a small leaving party for our colleague. There will be some nibbles still left if you come soon enough."

I was not pleased but there was no point in talking to her any further. I was not interested in the nibbles offered but I did walk to the X-ray Department fast.

The locum Registrar was an affable character who was just doing a weekend locum in between jobs. He had told me that his experience was mainly in Neurological Surgery and his Orthopaedic knowledge was a bit 'rusty'.

I had clear evidence of that on the previous evening when he was doing an emergency hip operation. I had to help him and show him how to insert the prosthesis in the shaft of the femur otherwise it would have been a disaster.

He was not arrogant and was very willing to cooperate with colleagues. Too willing perhaps; that was why he readily agreed with the Radiographer that there was no need to do the X-rays I had requested.

When I saw him I told him in no uncertain terms, "If you want to discharge this patient from the casualty Department without doing these X-rays, feel free to do that. You will have to go and see her and write in the notes. It will be your responsibility then."

The man didn't expect this turn of events. He said, "No, no. If you feel so strongly about it, let us get them to do the X-rays."

There was no further reluctance from the Radiographer. The leaving party for her friend was over by then anyway!

The open mouth views showed that the teenager had a fracture of the odontoid process without displacement. If not properly fixed to allow it to heal it would be extremely dangerous; she could be paralysed from neck down! I told the Registrar that he had to inform the Consultant on call about this case. He promptly did so. Mr Prior came immediately and a 'halo fixation' was done to immobilise her neck completely. It was certainly an unpleasant ordeal to the patient, but far better than a permanent paralysis from neck down.

This incident taught me the importance of taking referrals from A/E seriously.

It also emphasised my belief that we have to argue our case and hold firm in the face of opposition to protect our patients from danger. Often their lives are in our hands.